"Talk to me, Ian. Tell me about your job, your life. I'm a good listener, you'll see," Trudy promised.

There was an openness in her expression, an eagerness to understand whatever he chose to tell her. There was also sympathy and kindness, both of which annoyed him unreasonably. "My job is to baby-sit you, whether I want to or not. That's my life," he said, walking to the door without giving her a second glance.

"I wish I'd known you before you were so angry at everyone," she said, stopping his exit.

"What makes you think I'm angry at everyone? How do you know it isn't just you I'm angry at?"

"Because I think you *like* me."

Trudy was so surprised when he grabbed her and clamped his mouth over hers that she gasped. Her body burned hot and molten, her world churned like the inside of an active volcano, full of fire and might.

Suddenly Ian pulled away. The passion in his eyes terrified Trudy, made her knees weak and her heart pound. He stared at her long and hard, struggling with emotions he'd never felt before. "You're right, Trudy," he said, his voice raspy. "But I like you just a little bit. . . ."

WHAT ARE *LOVESWEPT* ROMANCES?

They are stories of true romance and touching emotion. We believe those two very important ingredients are constants in our highly sensual and very believable stories in the *LOVESWEPT* line. Our goal is to give you, the reader, stories of consistently high quality that may sometimes make you laugh, sometimes make you cry, but are always fresh and creative and contain many delightful surprises within their pages.

Most romance fans read an enormous number of books. Those they truly love, they keep. Others may be traded with friends and soon forgotten. We hope that each *LOVESWEPT* romance will be a treasure—a "keeper." We will always try to publish

LOVE STORIES YOU'LL NEVER FORGET
BY AUTHORS YOU'LL ALWAYS REMEMBER

The Editors

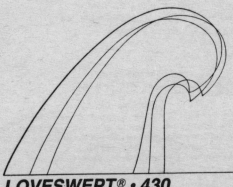

LOVESWEPT® • 430

Mary Kay McComas
Favors

 BANTAM BOOKS
NEW YORK • TORONTO • LONDON • SYDNEY • AUCKLAND

FAVORS

A Bantam Book / October 1990

LOVESWEPT® and the wave device are registered
trademarks of Bantam Books, a division of
Bantam Doubleday Dell Publishing Group, Inc.
Registered in U.S. Patent
and Trademark Office and elsewhere.

If you would be interested in receiving protective vinyl
covers for your Loveswept books, please write to this
address for information:

Loveswept
Bantam Books
P. O. Box 985
Hicksville, NY 11802

ISBN 0-553-44061-6

Published simultaneously in the United States and Canada

Bantam Books are published by Bantam Books, a division
of Bantam Doubleday Dell Publishing Group, Inc. Its trademark, consisting of the words "Bantam Books" and the
portrayal of a rooster, is Registered in U.S. Patent and
Trademark Office and in other countries. Marca Regis-
trada. Bantam Books, 666 Fifth Avenue, New York, New
York 10103

PRINTED IN THE UNITED STATES OF AMERICA

OPM   0 9 8 7 6 5 4 3 2 1

Believing that what comes
around should go around . . .

This book is dedicated to my agent,
Denise Marcil.

Prologue

The two chairs on the wide front porch creaked and groaned as the occupants rocked back and forth in nervous agitation. The old man had a white-knuckled grip on the arms of his chair, while the woman quietly wrung her hands in her lap. The stranger stared at them intently.

"Well now, Mr. Walker. I can't say that I've ever had a need to hire a mercenary before. Just how does one go about it?" the old man asked.

"I told you before, Mr. Babbitt. I'm not a mercenary," Walker said. "I'm an agent of the United States government. I'm here as a favor to your nephew, George Phillips, but if you'd rather get someone else to do the job, that's fine with me. I wasn't too crazy about taking it on in the first place."

"Oh my. Please don't take offense, Mr. Walker," the old woman said. "Our Trudy needs you. We've hired bodyguards through an agency, but they just don't seem to be working out. We went to George because we didn't know who else to turn to for help. If George thinks you're what we need to keep Trudy safe, then, well, we'd be very grateful for your help."

George Phillips was not only Walker's immediate superior in the agency, he was also his oldest and closest friend. It was a relationship that was frequently strained yet had always managed to stand up under the pressures they'd both exerted on it. Until now.

Walker knew the exact reason George had sent him to the Babbitts, and he knew that it had very little to do with keeping their granddaughter safe. He'd scratched the sensibilities of some very powerful people, made them mad as hell, actually. It was George's way of rapping his knuckles, and Walker resented being there.

"She belongs in a witness protection program," he said.

"That's what George said. Even the United States prosecuting attorney said so," Mr. Babbitt admitted. "But Trudy wouldn't have anything to do with it."

"The man she testified against actually said he'd hunt her down, that he'd find her and kill her. Can you imagine that, Mr. Walker?" Mrs. Babbitt asked. "Trudy worked for Claude Packston for several years before all this happened, and she doesn't seem the least bit afraid of his death threats. And she says she won't spend the rest of her life running from a man who's locked up in prison. Trudy says she ran and hid once before and lost everything." The woman glanced at her husband. "We're not sure what she means by that, but she refuses to take on a new identity or protect herself in any way."

They both looked up at Walker, who was leaning in a relaxed yet inherently menacing position against a tall white pillar, one leg bent carelessly over the railing, his hands in his pockets.

"The hearing is scheduled to take place two weeks from tomorrow," the old man said. "If Packston gets a new trial, they'll take Trudy into custody like they did last time. If the appeal is denied, she won't be any worse off than she was after the first trial."

"Will you watch out for her, Mr. Walker? Until we get the results of the hearing? Mr. Compton, the man who's watching her now, is terribly eager to quit, and she needs someone to take care of her for at least the next two weeks, maybe three. After that we're just not too sure of what'll happen."

"Why is Compton so eager to leave? Sounds like pretty easy money to me," Walker said, mildly curious. It didn't make any difference to him why the man wanted to leave. He had a debt to pay to George Phillips. He'd baby-sit Trudy Babbitt and call it even with George—if he didn't die of boredom first.

"Apparently there's some sort of personality conflict with Mr. Compton. Trudy likes him, but she thinks he'd be happier working for someone else. He's sent us reports. Would you like to see them?" Madge Babbitt asked, implying that if he did wish to see the papers, he was as good as signing a contract to protect her granddaughter with his life.

He looked at the two elderly people. The desperation, fear, and worry in their faces were familiar to Walker. He hadn't yet grown immune to such expressions.

His lips curved into a brittle half-smile.

"Sure. I'll take a look at them."

One

The drive across the mountains to the small town of Victory was uneventful and shorter than Walker had anticipated. The Babbitts had promised to call ahead and let Compton know that he was on his way, but he wasn't about to report in and take over his new assignment one second earlier than was absolutely necessary.

Assignment, ha! He felt like a naughty first grader being sent to stand in a corner.

As he turned onto the street he'd been looking for, a big white house with a wraparound porch came into view, bearing the numbers listed on the slip of paper in Walker's hand. It had royal blue shutters with a matching front door. It looked tidy and well kept; the yard was a profusion of multicolored flowers.

"Oh, jeez," he muttered along with some other more colorful expletives as he pulled over to the curb. "It looks like Beaver Cleaver's grandmother's house."

There was a slim young woman tending the flowers that grew along the walk that led to the house. She looked like someone out of an early fifties movie with her broad-brimmed hat and her fluffy floral-print dress. The whole scene looked like a throw-

4

back to another era, and it made Walker's stomach roll over in despair.

In a knee-jerk reaction, he pressed his foot down on the accelerator, and the car went speeding down the road. Procrastination wasn't normally a weakness he gave in to, but in this situation he felt it was justified. Humiliation was not something he enjoyed.

He spotted a small park and pulled over. He needed to gain some control, find a facade to hide behind. He'd be damned if he'd let the whole world see how irritated he was over being treated like a child, like a bad little boy.

He got out of the car and walked over to a bench near the center of the park. Sitting down, he stretched out his long legs, crossing them at the ankles. The level of his anger and frustration was so high, he didn't pay much attention to the figure approaching him. Why should he? he asked himself. He was in the land of the free and the home of the brave and in no danger from his enemies any longer. Not to mention the fact that he was in some rinky-dink town, where no one knew who he was or cared. There was no need to keep his guard up until he went to work again—if baby-sitting could be called work.

"Oh, no!" a high-pitched female voice exclaimed.

Walker turned his head to see a pint-sized woman, her arms loaded with twigs and tree branches, doing a slapstick balancing act as the tree parts teetered and slipped away from her one by one. She bent to pick up two and lost three more. Walker could see she was fighting a losing battle, and even as leery as he was of being of any assistance to anyone at that moment, he got grudgingly to his feet and ambled over to help her.

She was dancing about with her bundle of sticks, her back to Walker as he bent to pick up a few of the smaller twigs she'd lost. When he looked up, she was above him, tripping over her own feet.

"Oh, no," she cried out again. "Look out."

Of course, she fell on him. Walker was having that sort of day—and he hadn't any hope of having a better one for a long, long time. He should have stayed on the bench.

She was laughing.

"This is certainly an interesting way to meet someone," she said, giggling, disentangling her slim, shapely legs from around his neck. "But you look even grumpier now than you did over on the bench. Are you angry?"

Walker looked up and stared into the most unique face he'd ever encountered.

He wasn't sure if it was caused by her present state of agitation or if it was natural, but the roses in her cheeks matched the rosy blush of her lips, giving her a healthy, vibrant appearance. And for some strange reason that had nothing to do with the way she looked, he kept thinking that he knew who she was. He would have sworn on a Bible that he'd never seen her before, and yet she stirred something familiar deep inside him.

"You are angry, aren't you? If you're not, you really shouldn't frown like that, because it makes you look really mad," she said as if she were commenting on the weather. She'd been watching for a man who looked dark and sinister, but her intuition told her that this man wasn't the one.

"Angry? Me? Why should I be angry? I took the risk of being a gentleman and trying to help you out with your . . . sticks here." He motioned to the twigs and branches scattered around them. "I guess I got what was coming to me."

"Oh, my. You really are an angry man. I thought so the moment I saw you sitting over there on the bench. I said to myself, 'Now, that looks like one very angry man to me.' And I was right," she said, getting to her feet. "I was going to steer clear of you and just leave you there to pout. I mean, it's not as if you're a friend of mine or anything, but you looked so unhappy. And while I was trying to make up my mind whether or not to talk to you, I lost my grip on my firewood and . . . well, here I am talking to you."

Walker stared at her, wondering how she managed to talk so fast and get to her feet at the same time when there was nothing but air and a pretty face between her ears.

Out of nowhere a rush of vague mental images and a sharp awakening of long-forgotten emotions held Walker immobile. Memories of a summer love came to him as vividly and breathlessly as if he were experiencing them for the first time.

He looked up into eyes that were a warm chestnut brown, and even though he remembered sky blue, he felt the same prickling sensations tickle through his body and settle low in his pelvis. At fifteen he'd thought golden curls were the direct result of having been touched by the gods, but his fingers were actually itching to touch the raven hair that framed the heart-shaped face before him. Pale white skin, flawless and smooth to the point of appearing like a fine figurine's, eclipsed his memory of a golden California girl.

The pixielike woman standing beside him conjured up the same wild and overwhelming physical excitement that had turned his life inside out and upside down when he'd been a youth on the brink of manhood. He swallowed hard. He felt confused and off kilter, feelings he rarely encountered and didn't relish at all. Who was this person? he wondered.

"Why are you staring at me like that?" she asked.

He shook his head, trying to ignore the turmoil inside him. "You're standing on my hand."

"Oops." She removed her foot, and Walker flexed his fingers, attempting to get the circulation back. "You aren't by any chance a forest ranger?" she asked. She smiled down at Walker, merriment glimmering in her eyes.

"Do I look like a forest ranger?"

"Well," she said, stooping to retrieve her firewood, not looking at Walker. "If you weren't being so sarcastic, and if I used my imagination, I think you'd make a very handsome forest ranger. But as it is, no, you don't look like a forest ranger. On the other hand, I don't need one right now anyway, so it doesn't really matter, does it?"

Walker had a feeling that he should agree with everything she said, at least until someone showed up with a leash for her.

"What are you going to do with all the wood?" he asked, intrigued by the way her hair shimmered in the late afternoon sun, showing not a mixture of colors but a pure jet black.

"It's for my campfire. I only have the one apple tree in my yard, and I didn't want to cut off branches just to burn them. And I understand that there's less smoke if the wood is old and dried out a bit. So I hiked over here to get some."

Walker was sorry he asked. He pressed his lips together to keep from asking how far she'd hiked; why she needed a campfire if she had a backyard, which would logically lead one to believe that she had a front yard as well and a house of some sort in between the two; and how long it would take her keeper to discover that she'd given him the slip? He didn't want to know. He didn't want to have anything to do with this person—not with her or with the way she could wreak havoc with his body. If he had to be on an imposed leave of absence from the rest of the world, why couldn't he just be left alone?

"Thank you," she said as he handed her the last piece of tinder for her fire. She stood again, staggering a little to get her balance, grinding his other hand into the ground with the soft heel of her tennis shoe in the process. If she heard him groan in pain, she didn't let on. She looked as if she were about to leave him there, no apology offered, when suddenly she smiled at him and said, "I hope that whatever's bothering you goes away soon. I've always thought that life was like a series of transitions and that once you've gotten through one of these changing periods, your life evens out a little and is better for a while. At least until it's time for your life to change again."

Walker was amazed not only by her brash speech but by her sincerity. Did she really believe that he gave a damn *what* she thought? She obviously did, because she went on talking.

"But I've also thought that these times of growing and becoming a better person were always very painful. I hope yours doesn't last too long."

He didn't know what to say, so he just nodded, pretending to agree with her again. She smiled, and her chestnut-color eyes twinkled at him warmly, as if he were her oldest, dearest friend.

Walker watched her walk away until she reached the street, and then he turned his back on her. He felt a heaviness, a constriction in his chest, and he knew that she had somehow caused it with her crazy talk. Or maybe it wasn't so much what she said as the way she'd said it, as if she truly cared.

He shook his head, then wiggled his whole body, trying to shake off the eerie feeling she'd given him. If he were slightly less cynical, he might have been able to believe she *was* some sort of pixie or something, sent to give him hope in an hour of need. As it was he simply suspected that her brain was pickled.

When procrastination turned to outright insubordination, Walker's ingrained sense of duty and commitment compelled him to get into his car and drive back toward the Victorian nightmare of a house where his next assignment as a highly trained and experienced government agent awaited him.

He parked the car across the street, resigned to his fate. He saw that the woman in the puffy dress and big hat was still gardening. Didn't she have anything better to do? he wondered. And in that dress yet? She'd had the time to horticulture those flowers to within an inch of their lives by now, he decided.

He ground his molars together, steeling his determination as he got out of the car and raised the lid of the trunk to retrieve his suitcase.

It was then that a movement at one of the windows on the upper floor caught his attention. He grabbed at a slim thread of hope that the man hanging out the window frantically waving his arms like a lunatic was not the bodyguard, Compton. But the thread eluded him, and he automatically took on Compton's agitation.

He dropped his bag back into the trunk and slammed down the lid. He bolted across the street and glanced up at the window in time to see Compton cautioning him to stay cool and to look casual, motioning at the woman below.

Obviously Compton didn't want the woman upset. Walker could live with that. Screaming, hysterical women had a tendency to get on his nerves. The situation didn't appear to be particularly menacing at the moment, or Compton wouldn't have cautioned him. Still, Compton's manner was insistent.

Hearing his steps on the sidewalk, the woman turned.

"Afternoon," he said, smiling, hoping to distract her enough to keep her from noticing Compton at the upstairs window. He felt forced to say more and act unhurried. "Nice flowers."

"Thank you." The woman rearranged the elastic at the end of each puffy sleeve before she looked directly up at Walker, using one hand to keep her umbrellalike hat in place. "Are you a friend of Fred's," she asked with a deep, raspy voice that Walker found provocative and lusty.

She was blond with smooth loose curls hanging to her shoulders. Her face was narrow with high, prominent cheekbones, full, soft lips, and pale blue eyes that seemed too big for her face. She looked frail and feminine and, Walker supposed, appealing—if frail and feminine were his style, which they weren't.

"Ah, yes. I am," he answered, unsure whether she'd seen Compton's antics or not. He tried to ignore the open, speculative stare that she passed over every inch of his body.

"Fred's room is at the top of the stairs on the left," she said with a slow, cloying smile that made Walker feel strange and nervous. "Mine's directly across the hall."

Walker's face froze in a half-smile, and he nodded. "Thanks."

Dear Lord, why me? he asked as he pulled open the screen door and walked into the house, filing away for later use the facts that the porch floor creaked and the screen door squeaked.

"Walker? Up here. Quick," Compton said from the landing at the top of the stairs which were located directly across a large foyer from the front door. "I don't want her to see me."

Walker scanned the premises as he crossed to the stairs with a long, brisk stride. "Who?" he asked, seeing no one else around.

"Her. That . . . that person out front."

Walker glanced over his shoulder at the woman on the sidewalk, who was indeed watching his ascent. When he reached the top step, Compton all but picked him up and threw him into the room on the left and quickly closed the door.

"What the hell took you so long?" he demanded. "You were supposed to be here two hours ago."

"I got hung up. What's the matter with you? What the hell is going on here, Compton?"

Compton expelled a huge breath, and sagged back against the closed door. From his rear pocket he pulled a large white handkerchief and mopped his damp forehead with it as he spoke.

"She's been after me for weeks now. I didn't know what else to do but quit the job. I tried everything.

But she just kept coming on to me and coming on. . . . She's dangerous," he said, distraught. "Walker, I can't tell you what I've been through."

With a disbelieving look Walker crossed to the window and looked down at the woman below. Her movements were graceful and elegant as she snipped dead blooms off the plants and pulled what few weeds grew up beside them.

"She does look pretty ferocious with those little garden snippers, Compton," he said facetiously. "Does she keep her Uzi under that hat?"

"Laugh, Walker." Compton was defensive and indignant. "Laugh all you want, but I'm the one who's leaving here. You're staying. By tomorrow afternoon you'll be laughing out the other side of your mouth."

Walker frowned, perplexed.

"Your report said she was being cooperative. And Fillmore's said she was a pleasant person. What's she been doing?"

"I said the Babbitt woman was being cooperative. That one down there is too cooperative, if you get my drift."

"I don't. Isn't that her there?"

"Her who?" Compton was getting more and more flustered by the minute. "There's four of them."

"What?" Walker exclaimed, confused and horrified at once.

"There are four women living in this house," Compton stated, exasperated. "The Babbitt woman runs this place. It's a boardinghouse. I can see those two old con artists didn't tell you any more than they told me when I signed on."

"Wait a second," Walker interrupted. "Is that Trudy Babbitt down there or not?"

"Not. That's Ruby."

"And she's hot to trot."

"It's more like trample you to death, but yeah, she's hot. Keep yourself moving when she's around, or she'll jump your bones so fast, it'll make your head swim."

"Well, where the hell is the Babbitt woman? She's the one you're supposed to be watching, Compton."

"That's true," Compton said. "But Trudy's nothing compared to that one."

"So? Where is she?"

"She's gone camping. If you'd gotten here when you were supposed to, you could have met her. Now you'll have to wait until tomorrow."

"Camping? For Pete's sake, Compton. Have you lost your mind?"

Compton shook his head, confident of his sanity. "Come on, I'll show you."

Walker followed Compton down the hall, away from the front of the house, and through an open bedroom door at the end of the corridor.

He thought at first it was a child's room, but on closer examination that impression simply didn't hold. Pillows, scarves, dolls, figurines, and hats dazzled him with their glorious colors. There were toys everywhere. Pictures and photographs covered the walls. It was an eclectic array of bright, colorful treasures obviously loved and carefully placed in a way that even the most fastidious child couldn't manage.

Walker amazed himself by releasing a soft laugh at the sight, not because it was humorous, but because he didn't know of any other way to react to it. Plainly, the room belonged to an adult female. It was the vivid colors and the toys that threw him. And yet, strange as it was, something about the room appealed to him, evoked something pleasurable in him.

"There," Compton said, pointing out the window.

Walker crossed the room, taking in plants, books, and needlework as he went. He stooped to peer out the window. Inside the fenced yard below was what appeared to be a campsite.

A small green tent was staked out under an old

gnarled apple tree. There was a small director's chair placed between the tent and a ring of stones, which was obviously a fire pit. There was no fire as yet, but the leaves and twigs were laid out meticulously in preparation, and there was a small pile of wood beside it.

But there was no camper in sight. No Trudy Babbitt.

"So? Where is she?" Walker asked. A sick feeling deep in the pit of his stomach told him that he'd recognize Trudy Babbitt on sight, that he'd already had an . . . encounter with her.

"In the tent."

"How can you tell?" He wondered what Compton would say if he told him that she'd just been over in the park gathering wood—alone.

"Listen."

Walker listened. He heard birds chirping and a soft summer breeze rustling the leaves on the trees. He picked out the sound of crickets, which he might have taken for granted if he hadn't heard the hoot of an owl and the sound of a frog croaking rhythmically in the distance. Something didn't jibe. Walker frowned at Compton.

Compton smiled back at him.

"What the hell is that?" Walker asked.

"Trudy." Walker's frown grew deeper, forcing Compton to explain. "What you're hearing is camping music." He chuckled delightedly. "Can't go camping without the right noises, you know."

Walker glanced down into the yard and then back at Compton. The man didn't appear to be joking. What's more, he was acting as if what he was saying wasn't at all unusual. "Cricket music," he muttered as his head hit the window frame with a loud thud.

"Actually, that's called 'Symphony of the Night.' Helena borrowed the tape from the library for her."

Never one to assume the worst of any given situation, Walker had to ask, "What does this Babbitt woman look like?"

Compton hummed, trying to think of just the right words. "She looks like a little Irish fairy," he said finally.

"A leprechaun?"

"No, Trudy's prettier, but she still has a magical look about her . . . like a little Irish fairy," he insisted. "You don't get tired of looking at her, you know?"

Walker was silent for several long minutes before he replied. "Look, Compton, I have some money socked away. Lots of money. I'll give it all to you if you stay and finish this job."

"No way, pal. It's all yours. I'm leavin'." And then, seeing the expression on Walker's face and taking pity on him, he added, "Look. It's not all that bad, Walker. Trudy isn't, anyway. She's easy to look at and as sweet as the day is long. You'll like her."

"I doubt it," he said, his assumption no longer unfounded. "I don't handle flaky women very well. I prefer women who use their brains."

Compton arched a brow. "Don't underestimate our little Trudy, Walker. I'll admit that she has her own way of doing things most of the time, but she's no flake. She's . . . unusual. Special."

"Right."

He didn't think it was necessary to tell Compton that he'd already met the little fairy, and he was spared the decision as Compton went on to explain the routine around the house.

He gave Walker a folder of background material on the other residents at the boardinghouse, and finally made his escape, leaving Walker to introduce himself to Trudy Babbitt.

Before availing himself on that dubious pleasure, Walker made a thorough inspection of all the rooms in the house. He cringed at all the broken locks on the windows and rolled his eyes heavenward when he discovered that there weren't any dead bolts on the doors. Hell, a three-year-old could get in and out of the place without the slightest problem, he realized. It wouldn't even be a fair contest to a professional hit man. Walker's head began to ache as a feeling of impending disaster came over him.

Two

"Ms. Babbitt? Trudy Babbitt?" Walker called from outside the tent as he listened to the hooting, croaks, and chirps on the tape recording. He took in the tidiness of the woodpile and kindling, wondering what kind of person would go to all the trouble of stacking it according to size.

When no answer came, he called out again, a little louder and stronger this time. Still getting no response, he bent at the waist and slowly parted the tarpaulin to peer inside.

"Ms. Babbitt?"

"Yes?" The voice came from directly behind him. It startled him. He hadn't heard her approach—something so unnatural to him that he turned, instinctively combat-ready.

"Oh my," Trudy cried, astonished and terrified by what she saw in his face. This *wasn't* the same man she'd met in the park. Could she have been so entirely mistaken? Was this the man? The killer? Her mind froze on that notion, and she automatically flinched defensively, taking a step backward into the studio chair and falling heel over head into the small woodpile.

Walker grasped the situation before the woman hit the ground. Unfortunately he couldn't grasp *her* in time to keep her from falling. "Dammit, lady. Don't you know better than to sneak up on someone like that," he bellowed, reacting more to his own fright than to her misdeed. "I could've killed you."

"I . . . I," she babbled, scrambling about, trying to untangle her legs from the chair. *I should have disappeared when I had the chance,* she told herself. *I shouldn't have set myself up like this. I should have moved out of the country, crawled in a hole, and buried myself. I'm not prepared. This isn't the way I thought it would happen. I'm going to die.* Her thoughts raced, and her frustration mounted as she desperately tried to extricate her feet from the chair and flee for her life.

Walker could see that she hadn't yet realized that she was in no danger. He could feel her fear and knew an uncharacteristic pang of guilt for having caused it. He stepped toward her and reached down to pick her up. He lifted her under her arms, the way he would a child, and shook the chair loose from her feet. He saw stars and tasted blood when her fist flipped up into the air, cracking him a good one on the chin.

"I'm not going to hurt you," he growled, his eyes watering from her punch.

Fighting, of course, was Trudy's first choice of defense, but being suspended a foot off the ground left her little hope of that. Trudy forced her body to go limp. If she had to die, she'd die with dignity.

"Are you okay?" Walker asked. She appeared so petite and harmless in her khaki shorts and yellow T-shirt. She looked up at him. Her eyes were wide with fear, yet her chin was tilted upward defiantly. She was afraid and struggling to be brave. Walker was impressed.

"Are you okay?" he asked again.

An owl hooted and frogs croaked.

Trudy tilted her head to one side and took her time studying his face.

He was such a dark person—long dark hair, dark

eyes, the dark shadow of his beard outlining a strong, square chin. His skin was deeply tanned, and his clothes were black, but it was the bleakness that surrounded him, emanated from him, that struck her. Just as it had in the park.

She realized then that the killer look on his face that had frightened her moments ago was no longer there. He still looked dangerous. There was no doubt about that. But Trudy was a person who lived on her instincts, and they were telling her that as menacing as the man appeared, he wouldn't hurt her.

"You . . . you didn't follow me here, did you?" It was more a statement than a question.

"No. I'm . . ."

"Please put me down, then," she said calmly. He did, and she immediately set the chair upright and began to restack the wood. "Poor Fred," she said, "he didn't have a very good time here, I'm afraid. I'm very sorry about that. I liked Fred. He was a good eater."

Great. She speaks in tongues too, Walker concluded. He hadn't made sense of a word she'd said.

"I'm sorry, ma'am. What's a good eater?" He had to ask. "And who is Fred?"

She placed the last piece of wood on the pile, which was neat and ordered according to size once again, and then started to crawl off into the tent, saying, "A good eater is someone who eats all his supper, and Fred is the man you're replacing. I thought you all knew each other." There was a brief pause. "But, then, I guess a bodyguard agency is a pretty big place. And you probably don't have company picnics or Christmas parties, do you? No offense, of course, but it's hard for me to picture a bunch of people with guns under their arms eating chicken wings and having three-legged races. Owls don't hoot this early in afternoon, do they?" The crickets and frogs fell suddenly silent. The tent bobbed and swayed as she moved around inside it, hardly taking the time for a second breath as she went on speaking.

"Christmas, I suppose, would be downright depressing. I liked Fred, but that Mr. Fillmore, the one who was here before Fred? The first one? He was a bit of a sourpuss. And you," she said, crawling back out of the tent and standing up to face him, "are very scary."

Walker's mind was swimming. He didn't know if he should deny the accusation, apologize, or give her mouth-to-mouth resuscitation to restore oxygen to her brain. He decided to take a moderate approach.

"I am Compton's replacement, but we don't work for the same agency. How did you know I was here to replace him?" he asked, as fascinated as someone might be watching a boa constrictor swallow a live mouse.

"Oh!" she said, startled. "You must be the mercenary, then." She laughed. "I think my grandparents have gone a little too far this time."

"I'm not a mercenary," he said, not for the first time that day, more than a little tired of explaining the difference. "I'm . . . ah, hell. I work for your cousin George. I'm here because I owe him a favor."

"That must have been some favor. I can't think of anything more boring than baby-sitting me. Quite frankly, I think my grandparents are wasting your time," she said. Walker was struck by her perceptiveness. "Did Fred happen to leave a message for me? I'd meant to say good-bye to him, but as you can see, I've been camping."

"Yes, I see that," he said, glancing around the campsite, his nerves beginning to tingle with impatience. "I . . . he said to tell you good-bye and good luck and that he was sorry he couldn't finish his . . . chores."

He stumbled over the last word, unsure of its correctness. Compton had said it was something between him and Trudy and that she'd understand, even though Walker didn't.

"Such a sweet man," she commented as she began to circle Walker, studying him critically. He followed her with his gaze, turning his head swiftly when she came to stand in front of him again.

Without a doubt she was the strangest person he'd ever met. Two months earlier he'd have stuck the barrel of his gun up her nose and demanded to know who she was and what she was up to. But he already knew who she was. She was an innocent, a victim, a witness he was sent to protect. And what was she up to? Walker couldn't, wouldn't hazard a guess.

She'd said that she thought he was scary, and yet she showed no fear of him after their initial confrontation. His own reaction to her felt very much like fear. His heart was pounding, his mouth was dry, and adrenaline surged through his veins, yet he knew she was no threat to him.

"Well," she said with a great sigh. "I can see we're going to have problems with you living here too."

"Oh? And why is that?" he asked, more than mildly curious.

"You're very beautiful," Trudy wasn't bashful, and she never told a lie or beat around a bush unless it was absolutely necessary.

"Beautiful?"

"Oh, I know, men don't like to be called beautiful. But Adonis was supposed to have been the most handsome of all men, and I've seen him described as very beautiful." She side-stepped him and started walking across the yard toward the house. "Actually, I think it has something to do with the overall appearance of a man rather than just his facial features. If he has big, broad shoulders and a lean, muscled body like yours, as well as a handsome face, then I think he's called beautiful."

Again Walker was sorry he'd asked. He was also rather curious as to why she didn't seem to be affected by him, if he was so beautiful. Many other women had been.

"It doesn't really matter anyway," she went on to say. "Helena isn't going to like the way you look at all."

"Who is Helena?"

"Charlotte's mother."

Of course. "Charlotte's mother?"

She turned the water spigot on and walked the stretched-out length of the garden hose to the end. There she began to fill two plastic buckets with water.

"Didn't Fred tell you?"

"He had a plane to catch and didn't have time to fill me in on everything," he said, wishing he'd taken the time to go over Compton's case file more carefully.

Walker frowned, shifted his weight from foot to foot, and tried to think straight. He wasn't good at talking in circles or listening to someone talk in circles. The way this woman spoke irritated him. However, she didn't seem to be doing it on purpose, and he needed to be as patient as possible with her. There was no telling how long he'd be stuck there. A good rapport between them could make all the difference in the world.

He shook the tension out of his arms and attempted to take one of the buckets of water from her to be polite. Water sloshed on the leg of his favorite dark slacks as her grasp remained firm and she refused to let go.

"Charlotte is one of your tenants, right?"

"They're a team."

"The mother and the daughter?"

"They're wonderful magicians. Or at least Charlotte is. Helena is her assistant."

Walker took a deep, calming breath and released it slowly as he watched her set the buckets down outside the tent, then crawl inside again.

"What does all that have to do with me being here?" he asked, speaking at the tent.

"Well," she said from inside, "Helena is very career-oriented. I think she's a little nervous that Charlotte will give up the act for the first good-looking man who comes along. She doesn't even let Charlotte associate with Roy. He's Ruby's brother?"

"Yes. I remember." According to Compton's report, Roy was a mysterious nocturnal creature who no one knew very much about. To Walker's way of thinking, they all—Helena, Charlotte, Ruby, Roy, and the Babbitt woman—sounded very strange, indeed. He caught himself longing to be back in the Middle East, where the people he associated with were dangerous but not necessarily crazy.

"And Roy wouldn't hurt a fly," she was saying as she backed out of the tent bottom first, dragging a cardboard box.

Walker couldn't help but notice the firmness of her buttocks and the perfect shape of her legs as she came out of the tent. The shorts she wore rode high up on her thighs to reveal a little of the soft flesh underneath, tempting Walker's sense of touch. He noted her slim waist and small, rounded breasts under the tight T-shirt and looked away to gain control of his thoughts.

"You, on the other hand, don't look harmless," she stated. "Helena isn't going to like you at all."

Not an exceedingly patient man to begin with, Walker finally gave in to his frustration.

"Who the hell cares if she likes me or not? This isn't a social visit, you know. I'm not here to win any prizes. I'm here to keep your butt from getting blown away because you refuse to enter a witness protection program." She looked up at him then, and he was well pleased to see that he'd finally gotten her full attention.

"It's probably better not to leave any food inside the tent, don't you think? That way the bears won't tear up your sleeping bag, trying to get to it," she said, turning back to her box and dragging it away from the tent.

Evading an issue that was too painful or too complicated to discuss was different from telling a lie or beating around a bush. Trudy also believed in an individual's right to privacy. Her motives for her actions were none of the man's business.

Walker, beyond frustration and growing angry, glanced around the perimeter to make sure they were alone. "Ms. Babbitt . . ."

She giggled. "Please call me Trudy. Nobody calls me Ms. Babbitt."

"Okay, *Trudy*. I think it's about time that I got a few straight answers from you." His voice was strained with exaggerated calm as he took her by the arm and firmly led her to the studio chair. He swung her around so quickly that her foot came up and kicked him in the shin before he plunked her down into it.

Trudy was a little taken aback by the sudden display of temper from her new bodyguard. All her answers had been as straight as she could make them. She was trying very hard to be as cooperative as possible. Quite honestly, this protection business was becoming increasingly tedious. Not for the first time did she wish that she'd never agreed to it.

"I want to know exactly what's been going on here for the past six weeks," he demanded, rubbing his lower leg absently. He braced his hands on the arms of the chair, putting his face within inches of hers. "All the stuff that didn't get into the reports. I want to know why you aren't in a government protection program, why there aren't any locks on the doors, and what the hell you're doing out here. And I want clear answers. Use one-syllable words if you have to, but give it to me simple and straight."

Trudy arched a fine dark brow and stared into the murky depths of his eyes for as long as she could. But she had to face facts, the man was twice her size and there was something raw, appealing and yet terrifying, about him. She couldn't outstare him.

She wasn't, however, about to let him jump down her throat with his boots on, for no good reason.

"I'll thank you not to speak to me in that tone of voice, Agent . . ." She looked back up at him inquiringly.

"Walker."

"Agent Walker," she repeated with a nod. "For one thing, I don't think I deserve it. I have been exceedingly tolerant of the people my grandparents keep sending here to protect me, when, in fact, I don't believe they are necessary. You'll never know how sorry I am that I walked in on Mr. Packston only seconds after he had the misfortune of killing his wife. I've wished a thousand times that I'd stayed in bed that day," she said with a sad shake of her head. "Be that as it may, when called upon to testify, I felt it was my duty as a good citizen to do so. Now, I'm sorry for that compulsion as well, because my grandparents and the people at the Justice Department have taken a simple little threat, made in a moment of passion no less, and blown it completely out of proportion."

Agent Walker looked at her in stunned silence.

"It's true," she went on emphatically. "I didn't feel at the time that Mr. Packston really meant to kill me. People say horrible things when they're angry. But I know Mr. Packston. I worked for him for several years. And although he did kill his wife in a rage, I'm sure that if he'd had the time to calm down a little that day, he never would have done it. I'm just as positive that once he had the time to think it over, he realized that I had no other choice but to testify against him. And surely after six months in prison he's calmed down enough to regret his hasty words during the trial." She paused. "Why are you looking at me like that?"

"I was just wondering if you were ever going to

get around to answering my questions," he said, sounding not angry but defeated.

"I was trying to explain why you have no right to walk into my camp and start shouting at me, Agent Walker. I haven't done anything wrong."

Trudy felt a little sorry for the man when he hung his head dejectedly and shook it back and forth. She was sure he was about to apologize for his rudeness when he opened his mouth to speak, but then he snapped it shut again and closed his eyes. A muscle in his cheek twitched furiously under the weight of his guilty conscience, and Trudy smiled at his show of ego.

Men had such huge bags of self-esteem to carry around all the time. And Agent Walker was no exception. Trudy could tell. She liked people and thought herself to be a very good judge of human nature.

Agent Walker was a very interesting man from what little she'd been able to ascertain so far. He was an angry man, a very angry man. But he wasn't really angry with her. He was mad at the whole world. He was hurting and lonely, lost in a place where he didn't want to be. Trudy instinctively wanted to soothe and comfort him. Pain and heartache were all too common, it seemed to her, and so unnecessary.

What a shame, she sympathized. For all his strength, Agent Walker was a gentle man. Both times he'd taken her into his hands he'd been firm but remarkably careful not to hurt her. More than once she had seen him struggling to understand and be patient with her, even though it was beyond him at this point. Everything seemed to be complex and complicated to him, maybe he wasn't geared to comprehending the simple and ordinary, she thought.

As a matter of fact, Trudy suddenly realized, it was entirely possible that Agent Walker needed more care and protection than she did.

"I know you haven't done anything wrong," he

said at last. His voice was deep, smooth, and controlled. "But I'm trying to do a job here, and I need to be aware of how things stand."

Trudy didn't want to test his temper any further, but she did prefer doing one thing at a time. Concentrating her attention wasn't her specialty, but Roy had advised her that method acting was a quick way to learn something, and she was determined to learn camping in a hurry.

"This couldn't wait until I get home tomorrow, could it?" she asked tentatively.

The muscle in Agent Walker's cheek was really twitching now, but when he spoke, his voice was amazingly low.

"And just where do you think you're going?"

"Well, as you can see, I've already gone. I'm on an overnight camping trip. And to tell you the truth, I'm finding it very hard to focus on more than one thing at a time. It disturbs my concentration. So, if your questions could wait until I hike back to the house in the morning, I'd be glad to give you any answers you need then."

Agent Walker stood back and covered his face with his hands. He rubbed briskly, and then smoothed back his thick dark hair, saying, "Okay. I give up. We'll do it your way for now. But I want your promise that you won't leave this yard. Not one step beyond the fence."

"I promise."

"And you need to get locks for the doors and windows."

"Number two on my list for tomorrow," she said, smiling at him, liking him more now that he was showing a little flexibility. "And if you're going to insist on watching me, I believe Fred was planning to sleep in my room tonight. He said he could keep a close enough eye on me from the window." She hesitated briefly. "Although, I believe he was also planning to stay awake all night. I can assure you that won't be necessary. I have Chowder with me, and he's a very good watchdog."

"Chowder?" he asked, looking around for a dog. "I haven't seen or heard a dog since I got here. Where is he?"

"In the tent, sleeping."

"So why didn't he bark at me?"

"He probably didn't hear you," she said logically. "He's Helena's dog, and I believe he's quite old. I borrowed him for the night so that Fred wouldn't have to worry about me while I was away."

Agent Walker was very good at masking his thoughts, Trudy realized. She couldn't tell what he was thinking at that moment. He just kept staring at her with those keen, dark eyes, not saying a word.

"All my guests are very nice people, Agent Walker. They'll be glad to help you get settled while I'm away," she said, not knowing what else to tell him, wanting him to leave. It was becoming more and more difficult to imagine herself deep in the woods with a tall, excessively good-looking man in dark business clothes standing in the middle of her camp.

"Do you want me to call you Agent Walker tomorrow?" she asked impulsively. Agent Walker was such a cold name. Surely he had a nicer name than that. "We called Fred Fred, and he pretended to be a handyman so he wouldn't upset my guests. Are you going to pretend to be something?"

"I thought a writer, maybe. They stick pretty close to their typewriters, and they don't go out a lot," he said absently. "You can call me Walker."

"Walker what? You can't just introduce yourself as Walker. You'll need a first name."

"It's Ian." He had such difficulty saying it, she almost didn't hear it. Wasn't he used to using his first name? she wondered.

"Ian," she said, testing the feel of it in her mouth. "I like it. Is that your real first name?"

"Yes."

"I'm glad. Well, if there isn't anything else that we need to settle immediately . . ." She flapped her arms at her sides as if she were trying to shoo him away. "Will you be able to find your way back to the house?"

Walker looked over at the large white structure some fifty yards away and nodded. "Yes. I think I can do that."

In a stunned state of unspent anger, Walker lumbered back to the house and let himself in through the back door.

I must have really screwed up this time. Somebody somewhere is really ticked off at me, he decided as he stood inside the screen door looking back at Trudy puttering around her campsite. George had scraped this favor off the bottom of the barrel.

Trudy Babbitt didn't need a highly trained federal agent to protect her. She needed an orderly and a padded room. Even his anger didn't seem to make much of an impression on her. And he'd seen grown men blanch with fear in the face of his temper. But, then, most of *them* had known what he was capable of. It had become increasingly obvious to him that Trudy Babbitt had no idea who he was or what he'd done.

That thought had taken a lot of the bluster from the wind in his sails. And for some reason he couldn't define, he was glad she didn't know. He hoped she never found out. She might believe he was a mercenary, but she had no real idea of what that entailed. Perhaps she was the one pure soul in the world who would never look at him with fear and suspicion in her eyes.

That was stupid. She didn't have the sense to come in out of the rain or protect herself from a very real danger that she'd been warned about. What made him think she'd have the sense to be afraid of him? he wondered, disgruntled.

Still, as inept as he thought Trudy to be, he couldn't deny the warm, peaceful feeling in his chest at that moment.

"I see you've met our little Trudy," a deep husky voice said from several feet behind him.

Walker turned to see Compton's hot blonde leaning in the kitchen doorway and muttered a vivid expletive. Twice in less than an hour he'd been unaware of someone approaching him from behind. What the hell was happening to him? If he didn't snap out of it, the Babbitt woman would end up dead, and he'd wind up on some streetcorner selling flowers to tourists.

"Yes. I met her."

"Did you enjoy your hike?" she asked, smiling. Although she was watching him with a decidedly sexual interest, there was a glimmer of humor and understanding in her eyes. Walker sensed that she knew the confusion and frustration he was feeling.

"Is she always like that?" he asked, ignoring her bold, calculating gaze.

"You think she's nuts?"

"I think she's halfway down that road, yeah."

"She's not, you know. In fact, she's probably got more marbles than the rest of us do." She breezed over to the refrigerator, her soft, flowing gown fluttering as she moved. "You're replacing Fred, I take it," she commented casually as she poured herself a glass of iced tea. When she turned to lean gracefully back against the counter, she saw the confusion in his face. She laughed. "You'll find us an unusual group of people, Mr. . . ."

"Walker."

"Mr. Walker. But none of us are particularly stupid. This is a small town, and most of us have lived here with Trudy for the better part of six months. Now, none of us thought too much about it when her grandmother called her every night to remind her to lock the doors and windows. We just thought she was a little different—like the rest of us. But when tall, good-looking strangers started appearing at the door and staying in the house with seemingly nothing better to do all day than follow Trudy around, well, even a bunch of idiots would eventually pick up on the fact that all was not as it appeared to be."

Ruby's words were the first that made sense to Walker all day. He pulled a chair away from the table and sat down facing her.

"So what's the general consensus?" he asked, amazed that he wasn't the slightest bit surprised or angry that everyone in the house had surmised that Trudy was under surveillance.

"That Trudy is in some sort of trouble," she said, shrugging an elegant shoulder, casting him a leery eye. "Fred never would admit that he was anything but a traveling handyman. Why aren't you denying anything?"

Walker couldn't resist laughing. "I guess because this is the first coherent conversation I've had since I got here," he said. "But I'm also not admitting to anything. I'm a writer. Freelance. I'm just passing through town, looking for an angle."

Ruby stared at him long and hard, then she shrugged. "Just don't let anything happen to her, okay? She's . . . somebody special."

With that, she put her glass in the sink and walked back to the door that led into the front hall. She turned, and in that deep, husky, suggestive voice she had, she said, "Of course, you know where to find me if you need any assistance . . . of any kind."

Walker's thanks-but-no-thanks grimace made her laugh as she walked down the hall and up the stairs to her room. He could certainly see how this woman could have gotten to Compton. She was the sort of female that would have a man constantly checking the fly of his pants to make sure it was securely fastened.

"Good-byyyyye, Trudy," two voices suddenly called out in unison from the back door, dragging their words out as if they had to cover a great distance.

Walker turned in time to see two women coming into the house, their attention focused out in the yard as they waved to the camper.

"Watch out for those bears," the younger of the two yoohooed loudly as the older woman froze in place at the sight of Walker sitting at the kitchen table.

Actually, it was probably a toss-up as to who was the most startled. Walker may have taken the woman off guard with his presence, but her huge orange hairdo and overly made-up face struck terror in his heart. He'd seen African tribal priests and witch doctors less frightening in appearance, less intimidating in expression. She was every child's nightmare, every grown man's horrifying image of a mother-in-law.

"Who are you?" she demanded, folding her arms over an ample bosom, bracing her legs under a bulky body. "And what are you doing here?"

A lesser man would have left the room. Walker stood weak-kneed to face her.

"Hello," he said in what he thought was a cordial tone. He held out a hand in friendship, much the same way he would to an unfamiliar and unfriendly dog. "My name's Walker. I'm a new boarder."

"Well, where exactly are you planning to sleep? The house is full." She turned to the younger woman who had come to stand behind her. "Trudy's been so preoccupied with her camping trip, she probably forgot and overbooked the place again. Remember the last time, when she had all those bums in blankets all over the floors?"

Walker deduced that the pair were the mother-daughter magicians. The daughter was pretty and blond and had a gentleness about her that she couldn't possibly have inherited from her mother.

"Mother, the shelter for the homeless had burned down. They had to go somewhere," Charlotte reminded her. "I thought it very kind of Trudy to let them stay here."

"They had bugs," Helena said, eyeing Walker intently.

"You don't have bugs, do you, Mr. Walker?" Charlotte asked encouragingly, a sweet, apologetic smile curving her lips.

"No," he answered through clenched teeth. He wanted to kill George Phillips.

"There you see, Mother? There's nothing to worry about, and I'm sure that when Trudy gets back from her camping trip, she'll settle the whole thing."

"Fred doesn't pay rent. He can have Fred's room."

"But where will Fred sleep?" She suddenly looked back at Walker. "Unless, of course . . . are you Fred's replacement?"

He opened his mouth to answer, and then closed it again. He wondered if the changing of the guard at Buckingham Palace got this much attention.

"Speak up, young man. Are you here to take Fred's place or not?" Helena wanted to know.

"Yes. I am." Why fight it? But if she asked to see his credentials or called him a mercenary, he was going to have the house evacuated.

She didn't. She even relaxed to the point of unfolding her arms. "I don't know why you didn't say so in the first place," she muttered, walking to the refrigerator. She began pulling things out of it, obviously well acquainted with its contents, then announced, "We have rules here, Mr. Walker. Dinner's at six sharp. Monday through Friday we take turns cooking, weekends we're on our own. We clean up after ourselves, and we do our own laundry. Saturdays we help Trudy with the cleaning and shopping, and we never discuss religion or politics. These are *single occupancy* rooms," she said, glanc-

ing at him knowingly. "And the bathrooms are first
come, first serve. We don't smoke in the house
and . . ."

The list of rules seemed to go on forever. Walker
looked across the table at Charlotte, who had taken
the seat directly opposite him, and found her smiling at him in a way that made him want to run
screaming into the night. How could this be happening to him? Trudy, whose attention he wanted,
could hardly be bothered with him, and yet every
other female in the house looked as if she wanted
him for breakfast—one way or another. He turned
his gaze back to Helena's broad form and didn't
move it again until he was free to leave the room.

As long evenings went, Walker's first evening at
the boardinghouse was the longest he'd ever known.

Dinner was good, though. Being a bachelor and
constantly on the move, most frequently in foreign
countries, he greatly appreciated home-cooked
meals. It had been Helena's turn to cook, and,
alarming as she was, the lady knew her way around
a pot roast.

It was the tension and the conspicuous lack of
table conversation that grated on his nerves.

All the boarders sat down precisely at six. Walker
was given Fred's place, between Ruby and where
Trudy usually sat at the head of the table. He could
tell by the looks he received that the gathered group
was eager to ask questions about him, about Trudy,
and about the circumstances they were in. But no
one asked.

Knives and forks grated on earthenware plates.
Dishes were passed. A digital clock on the sideboard
announced the time at the half hour in a computer-
ized monotone, and at one point Charlotte wondered aloud as to how Trudy was doing, all alone on
her camping trip. Eventually they all excused themselves, helped clear away the dishes, and went about

their normal routines. All the while they watched Walker closely but rarely spoke to him.

Walker knew he could have made the situation a little easier on everyone. He could have made up some plausible story to satisfy them. Hell, at this point he probably could have told them the whole truth. But he wasn't used to explaining his actions or asking for the cooperation of those around him. He did what was necessary to get a job done. That was how he'd been trained.

Trudy roasted marshmallows for as long as she could stand it. She couldn't see the point in setting sugar on fire and then eating it. But she'd heard it was a favorite pastime of children, a must on any camping trip.

This was one of the few times she regretted being raised by her grandparents, who'd both been well into their fifties by the time Trudy had gone to live with them as a nine-year-old. They were kind, gentle people, and Trudy loved them dearly. But camping had never been high on the list of things they'd wanted Trudy to experience.

She had no clear recollections of her parents. They had died together in a plane crash on their way to Zimbabwe on a missionary tour almost twenty years earlier. Her grandmother had told her they had been childhood sweethearts, in love with each other from the first glance. It followed, then, that they had loved her just as dearly, and she had always taken great comfort in that knowledge. At least she had always assumed that to be the case. Just as she assumed that they would never have approved of her eating burnt marshmallows.

She slipped another carbon-coated clump of sticky gook off the end of her stick and tossed it out into the yard, well away from the tent so as not to attract bears. She wasn't sure if bears liked burnt sugar or not, but she wasn't willing to take any chances.

Bears, however, weren't her only concern. There was also Agent Walker. Ian.

He'd been standing behind the screen door on the back porch for hours now, watching her every move. She was trying to ignore him. Her other overseers had been just as diligent at first. She knew his protectiveness would wear off when he came to realize just how calm and unthreatened her life really was.

But she soon learned that he was not to be ignored. She was acutely aware of him and of a feeling that there was something different about him.

For one thing, he was without a doubt the most handsome man she'd ever seen, she admitted, getting up to put the fire out. Fortunately she was intensely familiar with her proclivity toward infatuation where handsome men were concerned. She knew all the signs. And she knew that she was already supremely attracted to him. Who wouldn't be? she asked herself, crawling into her sleeping bag completely dressed except for her shoes, one of the many helpful camping tips Roy had given her.

She sighed. Ian was very handsome, so tall, so strong, broad in the shoulders. She had a real fetish for broad shoulders—big hands with long, graceful fingers. Ian had all these traits. She'd noticed them right away. Thinking of him made her heart race and gave her that sudden lifting and curling feeling deep and low in her abdomen. It was a wonderful sensation.

Oh, yes. She knew the signs, and she knew she'd have to be very careful. She'd have to remember that Ian was just passing through, she reminded herself, snuggling into her sleeping bag, wishing it smelled more like pine needles than of the dry cleaners.

"Ugh."

Trudy heard the noise in a half-sleep and came immediately alert. She wasn't sure what it was, but the sound had disturbed the rhythm of the crickets and frogs she'd been listening to all night and forced her back to a state of awareness.

Chowder apparently had heard nothing. He was curled up in one corner of the tent, sleeping soundly.

"Sssssht . . ." She heard what she thought to be a curse, hissed violently from several feet away from the tent. It never mattered how many times she told people out loud or whispered in her mind that she wasn't afraid; in her heart she was as she had always been, a coward. She wanted to run and hide just as she had so many years before. Running away had been easy. It was living with the consequences that she had found intolerable.

Her breath caught in her throat as she slipped her hand under her pillow and wrapped her fingers around the only protection she had against man or beast, and then waited and listened.

She couldn't see shadows through the thick fabric of her tent, but at odd intervals and between owl hoots she thought she could hear footsteps approaching. Slowly and quietly, so as not to disturb the sleeping Chowder, she turned herself around so that she was facing the opening of the tent. She waited and heard nothing but her own heartbeat throbbing in her ears.

She raised her weapon in one hand, and with the other she pushed one flap a fraction of an inch from the other and peered out into the darkness. She saw nothing. Boldly she widened the space between the flaps, and then suddenly—

"Holy hell and . . ." Trudy instantly recognized the voice but not all the words that burst forth the second her trigger finger took control.

"Ian? Agent Walker?" She scrambled out of the tent while the silence was filled with continued expressions of his pain and his present thoughts on her character.

"Oh, my goodness," she said, matching his agitation. "Let me help you. Why didn't you call out?

Move your hands away. I wouldn't have had to use my Mace if you'd called out and let me know you were coming. It was very foolish of you not to, you know."

"Get away from me. You're crazy."

"Keep your hands down, Ian. No, let me look." And then, quite put out in her own right, she said, "Oh, I can't see a thing. And I suppose all the rangers have gone to bed by now. I'll have to take you back to the house myself, I guess."

Blind and in excruciating pain, Walker groped the air for her neck. If he caught it, he planned to wring it tight.

"What the hell are you doing to me, lady? I'm blind. I can't see anything. Damn, it hurts. Get away from me. Just stay away," he shouted at her, his eyes stinging, his face on fire.

"Hush now," she said sternly. "I can only guess at how painful it is, but it won't help to be nasty. Here, put your arm around me and try to stand up."

"Nasty?" he asked, his deep voice deceptively quiet. He was on his feet. His hands fumbled over her body, grasping at her shoulders. "You call this nasty? Wait until I can see to aim my gun again."

"Yes, yes," she said absently, not bothering to impress Walker with her fear. He took a step toward her, bent on inflicting some pain of his own, but collided chest to breast with her instead, throwing them both off balance. "Oops. Careful now. Just follow me. Ugh, your hands are sticky. What have you been into? No, you can't hold my neck like that, it's hard for me to breathe. Just hold my hands, and I'll lead you. We'll rinse your eyes and have you feeling better in no time."

He hurt too much to argue with her. He'd kill her later, when he could see her better and enjoy the sight. She chattered the whole time it took them to get into the house, and Walker was very sensitive to the fact that between her directions and admonishments, she never once tried to apologize for spraying him in the face with her can of Mace.

"Oh my. What a mess," she said just inside the kitchen door. Walker was having a hard time keeping up with her, his shoes were sticking to the floor. "We'll have to take your shoes off."

"Why?"

"Because they have grass and leaves stuck to the bottoms of them and . . . ugh, marshmallow all over them."

This news didn't faze him a bit; it seemed par for the course.

Three

It wasn't until after he'd splashed tepid water into his face, and his eyeballs were merely throbbing and scratchy with his eyelids puckered against the overhead light, that he realized she felt no guilt at all for what she'd done. How much time had gone by since he'd stood on the back porch thinking her to be the sweetest, most innocent-looking woman he'd ever seen? An hour?

He squinted at her, his face raw and tender, wishing he felt up to teaching her a lesson. As it was, he felt sick.

"How many fingers do you see?" she asked when she noticed him trying to focus his eyes.

"Two . . . one . . . four." He finally pushed her hand away from his face.

"Bend your head back," she told him, her hands on either side of his face. "These eye drops might help take some of the red out. Goodness, you look awful, Ian."

"Thank you. You look like a blur." She didn't anymore, but he wanted to strike just one little spark of remorse in this woman before he kissed those soft, full lips of hers. Not that he really would—kiss her, that is. His list of reasons not to started with unprofessional and ended with she's nuts. But the urge to kiss her was definitely there, like a knife in his ribs.

He couldn't help himself. While he sat on the lid of the commode, she leaned over him, pressing cool compresses to his face and eyes, brushing his hair aside with her fingers, and smelling sexy as hell.

"Don't you ever get uncomfortable, wearing that gun all the time?" she asked, giving it a disapproving grimace.

"No."

She shrugged, and then she straddled his leg with hers, grazing his inner thigh as she positioned herself to administer the eye drops. It was an awkward pose at best, and when she teetered, Walker placed his hands on her hips to steady her.

"There. Better?" she asked, smiling down at him, showing him white teeth that were slightly uneven.

Lord, she was cute, he thought once again as he deliberately left his hands on her softly rounded hips.

"No," he said, never one to be a good sport. "But an apology might help."

She laughed. The sound tinkled in the air like chimes in the wind. "You're a stubborn man, Ian Walker. You still think this is all my fault."

"Not all of it, just most of it. A little sympathy would be nice too."

Again she laughed, and then she said, "Well, I suppose it would be. But to tell you the truth, I've been too busy feeling lucky to think much about it."

"Why lucky?" Had she known how close he'd come to killing her?

"Because this is usually the sort of thing that happens to me. Normally I'd have pressed the button and sprayed myself in the face. I got lucky tonight." She paused thoughtfully, paying little attention to Walker's sarcastic rebuttal. "Well, maybe not. I did blow my camping trip. That wasn't so lucky."

"What. Don't tell me you think you're jinxed."

"Oh no," she said, surprised that he'd say such a

thing. "It's nothing like that. That's a lot of non-sense anyway. It's just that . . . things just sort of happen to me sometimes. Some good, some not so good, and enough really rotten things to make me grateful for the things that aren't so rotten. But I never have any control over them, you know? They just happen. Granny says I have a knack for being in the wrong place at the right time."

"You mean the wrong place at the wrong time."

"No. I mean the wrong place at the right time." He obviously didn't understand. While trying to find the words to explain it, Trudy sat down in a most natural and unconscious way on Walker's leg. The relief she'd felt upon discovering Ian as her stalker had been swallowed up in her efforts to ease his pain and was only now taking its toll on her. She was suddenly weak and extremely tired.

Walker didn't blink, didn't move a muscle when he felt her soft, round bottom nestle down on his thigh. But he did do a mental review of all his reasons not to grab her and kiss her until she went limp in his arms.

"Granny says, and I do believe she's right in her thinking about this, that everything happens for a good reason. Like my walking in on Mr. Packston. I was definitely in the wrong place, but it was the right time, because he needed to be caught, and I needed to testify against him. See how it works?"

"It's still a little blurry," he said, taking on the role of devil's advocate. "Give me a good reason for shooting yourself with Mace. What if you hadn't been so lucky tonight? What good could have come from that?"

"I don't know. Nobody does until after it happens. And most of the time the reason isn't clear at first. But say I did it," she suggested, enjoying the conversation. "Say I sprayed the Mace in my face and had a horrible reaction to it. I go blind. That would be pretty terrible, wouldn't it?"

He tried to visualize her warm, sparkling eyes

without expression, sightless. The exercise twisted at something in his chest.

"Unbearable."

"That's right. And then I'm so filled with despair that I become desperate to see again. After a few years I discover this very strange little doctor with a big red nose and a drinking problem, who is an outcast in his profession, but who also thinks he can cure me, and I let him do experimental surgery on my eyes."

"You'd do that?"

"If I were desperate and filled with despair, I might. And what if he has developed a wonderful technique that no one else thought would work but in actuality worked beautifully and restored my sight. And it could restore the sight in thousands of other people as well. Then wouldn't it be a good thing that I shot the Mace in my eyes instead of yours?"

"Is your middle name Pollyanna?"

"Are you laughing at me, Agent Walker?" she asked, taking exception to the label.

"Absolutely not." How could he laugh? With her bottom on his knee and her legs astride his thigh, he didn't dare laugh for fear the joke would be on him. "But I didn't go blind, and you can bet your bu . . . buttons that I'd never let that character you described anywhere near my eyes. So where's the good in my getting the Mace?"

"We don't know yet," she said simply. "Maybe it was for this little talk we're having. Because I like you much better now that I know I can talk to you without you yelling at me."

"Maybe," he said, wondering what harm could come from one little kiss. It would certainly take the edge off the tension deep in his belly. "I'm feeling a little better about you, too, I guess."

"There, you see?"

Their gazes met as they smiled at each other in a more than friendly manner. Ah! Trudy loved this part. The first kiss was *always* the best. The sizzles and sparks or the lack thereof in the very first kiss could either make or break a relationship. And she had a feeling that the kiss she was about to share with Ian was going to light up the sky like the Fourth of July.

For a man used to getting things done in the quickest and most efficient way possible, the waiting he'd endured to touch Trudy's hair and skin seemed more like eons than hours. But he wasn't disappointed. Skin as smooth and delicate as a rose petal warmed the palm of his hand as he encircled her neck. Hair as thick and soft as the pelt of a mink brushed his knuckles while he lost himself in the depths of her eyes.

Somewhere in the back of his mind he knew that what he was doing and feeling was crazy. How could he want a kiss so badly? Trudy's kiss. What was it about her that tied his guts in knots so tight they ached?

Trudy watched as his face drew closer to hers. She saw the desire and speculation in his eyes. She felt her heart quicken, felt it throbbing in her throat and pounding in her chest. His fingers on her skin were like fire . . . and then, suddenly, everything was different.

"Ian," she whispered, panicky.

"Shhh."

She felt the heat of his breath against her lips and knew that Ian's kiss would change her somehow. In that instant she sensed that their first kiss would be like no other. It would be more than curiosity, more than the fulfillment of a need, more than the satisfaction of a mutual attraction and much, much more than she was prepared for.

"Are you people just about finished in there?" Helena's voice boomed through the bathroom door. "Some of us are trying to sleep, you know?"

Walker sat straight up on the toilet, his hands slipping back down to Trudy's hips when he heard her say, "Oh, Helena. Come in here for a minute, will you? I want you to look at Ian's eyes and tell me what you think."

Helena was a living scream of horror in her long blue terry robe and fuzzy slippers. Her craggy face was without makeup, and her orange hair was no longer in residence atop her head, which was now sparsely covered with thin gray tufts.

She took in Trudy's dazed expression and her position on Walker's knee with a frank stare. And while Trudy gave her an in-depth report of the proceedings, Helena silently moved Trudy aside and peered down into Walker's eyes.

Aged and seasoned gray eyes assessed the damage and then continued to assess the man. Her final judgment wasn't evident in her facial features when she finally declared, "He'll do fine." She turned to Trudy. "Why didn't you call one of us rangers to come rescue him. Your camping trip is ruined."

"I thought you were all asleep," Trudy said, amazed at the relief she was feeling. It wasn't like her at all. She liked kissing handsome men more than she liked Christmas.

"So, what'll you do now? You can't take them camping if you don't know what you're doing. You'd get them all killed."

"Well, I think I got a pretty fair idea of what the weekend will be like. Now I just need to remember not to volunteer to do it again. I'm not too crazy about camping. But a promise is a promise, and you're right, I still don't know what I'm doing. It just wasn't working out in the backyard. I need the real thing." She was thoughtful for a moment, and then she said, "I think I'll go up this weekend alone. Get a real feel for it, you know?"

Walker had been following this conversation with a frown on his face. "What's all this about? Why are you camping if you don't like it?" he asked.

"In the interest of making a long story short, Trudy's taking a bunch of Sunshine girls on a weekend camping trip," Helena spoke up, yawning widely. "She's been method-acting a camping trip in the backyard because that fool Roy told her it was the best way to learn how to camp. Although, why she'd take any advice from him is beyond me."

That answered a thousand of Walker's nagging questions, and he wondered why he hadn't asked Helena about it before. If anyone would give him a straight answer, she would.

"I really wish you wouldn't talk like that about Roy," Trudy said, smoothly moving the conversation away from the camping trip. "He's really very nice, once you get to know him."

"And when exactly are we supposed to do that?" Helena wanted to know. "He sneaks in and out of the house at all hours of the day and night. He never talks to anyone except you, apparently. All I know about him is what his sister's told me, and, quite frankly, I think she's about two bricks short of a full load most of the time too."

"Oh, pooh. Neither one of them are. As a matter of fact—"

"Could we get back to this camping trip?" Ian asked in a rather bored tone of voice, his elbow braced on the tank of the toilet. Both women turned on him as if he were too much to be dealt with, but he went on undaunted. He spoke directly to Trudy in a distinct and concise manner. "You're not going camping this weekend."

His mind was made up on the subject. His decision was final.

But Trudy didn't know that.

"Of course I am. I promised I'd take them. The real campout isn't until after the hearing, of course, but I need the practice. And if"—she glanced quickly at Helena and then back to Ian—"if something comes up, say, if I have to leave town suddenly or something, well then, other arrangements will have to be made. But for now, all systems are go."

"The hell they are. For all you know, there could

be a hit man out there, paid and ready to blow you away at any moment. Your life's in danger, Trudy. You can't go traipsing off into the woods. There's no way I can protect you out there." He felt no qualms speaking freely in front of Helena. There was no point in his pretending to be anything other than what he was, when no one in the house was buying his story anyway. They had a right to know they were in just as much danger as Trudy.

"The girls' leader is eight months pregnant. She can't take them, and even though I haven't had much experience dealing with children, I like them and they seem to like me. All the girls have mothers, of course, but for one reason or another, they're unable to go. I have the time. So I'm the most logical choice."

"Trudy doesn't know how to say no," Helena answered, indicating this was Trudy's greatest character flaw.

"Besides," Trudy said, "if I needed protection, which I don't think I do, you'll think of a way to manage it."

"That was a direct appeal to your ego, Mr. Walker. How did it work?" Helena asked with her arms crossed over her bosom and her stern expression more exaggerated.

"Not too well. You don't think she should go either, do you?"

"Well, I'm not one for doing things for other people in the first place, but, no, I don't think she should go. Especially if she's in some sort of danger."

"I'm not in any danger," Trudy insisted, angry that they were ganging up on her. "It's too late now, anyway. I promised the girls. And that's that."

Trudy wasn't much of a person to argue. She didn't like raised voices, and once she'd made up her mind to do something, she always saw it through. Her grandfather had gone to a lot of trouble to instill this quality in her, and Trudy had always been proud of it.

When Ian's voice began to reverberate off the tiles in the bathroom, Trudy had simply walked away. She felt bad when he bumped into the wall, trying to follow her, but she'd made her decision. His bellowing wasn't going to do anything but wake up everyone in the house.

She took pity on him when it became obvious that his depth perception wasn't completely restored as yet. He rammed full tilt, facefirst into her bedroom door, insisting that he'd stay up all night and continue to check on her if she returned to her campsite. She hadn't been too thrilled about sleeping out of doors anyway. She didn't mind saving that experience for Saturday night.

Sometime later, long after she'd snuggled down into her soft, warm bed, she heard a door squeak down the hall. She listened as Ian stealthily crept into her room, closed her bedroom window, and snuck out again. And for a long while after that she lay awake, wondering if he was sleeping with his pants on in case anything happened. Or would he come streaking into her room naked if she let out a piercing scream? That scenario had many erotic possibilities she discovered in her dreams throughout the night.

Two hours later Walker shucked his clothes and got back into bed. All the evidence was in. It wasn't a boardinghouse, it was a nuthouse.

He'd just settled into a light sleep after securing the subject in her room, when he thought he'd heard something from the floor below. He'd known Helena wasn't up again, because the now-familiar sound of her stentorian snoring was still rattling his walls. He hadn't seen Charlotte or Ruby since dinner, and he hadn't even met Roy. And though their bedroom doors were closed and he had assumed them to be in bed, asleep, he had listed them as unaccounted for as he made his way to the first floor.

With scalpel-sharp senses he'd explored the first floor in the dark. When the digital clock in the dining room announced the time to be three o'clock, he had come very close to shooting it. His nerves were stretched and on edge, relaxing only a little when he saw a light and heard whispered voices coming from the kitchen. Hit men didn't usually need to turn on the lights. Still, his gun was drawn and his trigger finger was tingling with tension when he pushed the door open and found Charlotte in the embrace of a man who looked very like Ruby.

All three of them stared at one another in surprise. Walker was amazed at how much Roy resembled his sister and to find the sweet, gentle Charlotte in his arms. The other two had their attention riveted on his gun.

"Do you two know what time it is?" Walker asked, lowering his gun to his side. "Better yet, do you have any idea how stupid it is to be prowling around the house at this hour when, as I'm sure you already know, I'm here to kill *anything* that goes bump in the night if it comes anywhere near Trudy."

"Oh. Yes. We knew that. We . . . ah . . . ." Charlotte stammered nervously.

"I work late. I always come home about this time of night. If you kill me, my sister'll sue ya, so you'd better get used to my coming and going at night," Roy said in a deep, husky voice that was almost identical to his sister's. He seemed confident and didn't feel the need to release his hold on Charlotte, now that he was no longer gazing down the barrel of Walker's gun.

"You're Roy, I take it." When the man nodded and called Walker by his name in return, he knew no further introductions were necessary. But of all the boarders, Roy was the least known, and Walker was curious about him. "What exactly do you do? This is a strange hour for shift work."

"I'm a musician. Piano, guitar, a little bit on a couple of horns. I work in a club about forty miles south of here."

"That's how we met," Charlotte added. "I sometimes do my act there. I met Roy, and we . . . sort of hit it off right from the first. Roy told Mother and me about this place."

"I see," Walker said.

"No. You don't. At least you don't see all of it." Charlotte was still agitated, he noticed, even after he'd lowered his gun. "My mother doesn't . . . approve of Roy. She's very protective, you see, and I—"

"Look," Walker interrupted, "I don't care what you two are up to. My only concern here is Trudy. Don't let anyone into the house except the present boarders until I give you the all-clear. Is that understood?"

"You really think someone's out to get Trudy?" Roy asked.

Walker hesitated briefly. Trudy had rejected the witness protection program; her identity was no secret. And if there was a killer looking for her, everyone between him and her was in danger. If Trudy hadn't told the boarders by now, they had a right to know and the freedom to stay or go.

"Hard to tell," he said finally. "The man she testified against is still making his presence known outside the prison. He's well connected. If he's had Trudy's grandparents under surveillance, he knows where she is. There's an appeal hearing in a couple of weeks, and if he's granted a new trial, Trudy will have to testify again. If not, he still might try to kill her out of revenge. Either way, I'd say she's in a hell of a lot of trouble and that the two of you ought to pack up your families and leave."

"But we don't have to leave, right?"

Walker shrugged and shook his head, letting his expression tell them how stupid it would for them to stay.

"Won't she ever be safe?" Charlotte asked, worry marring her sweet, angelic features.

"I'm not sure," he said truthfully as a cold shiver raced up his spine. "We'll know more after the hearing." He paused thoughtfully as something else began to nag at him. Turning his attention to Roy, he asked, "Are you and your sister twins?"

"No. But our parents were very close."

"Cute." He drew a breath and was about to tear into Roy when Charlotte hastily stepped in.

"My goodness, Mr. Walker. What happened to your eyes? They look just awful. Do they hurt? They must," she said, deciding on her own. "They look terrible."

"Thanks." He turned and walked out of the room. He didn't have the energy to take care of Roy's smart mouth or Charlotte's redundant questions. He'd have George Phillips do some more checking into the background of all the boarders in the morning, he decided as he returned to his bed.

He lay with his arms folded back behind his head and watched the night shadows flicker across the light fixture in the center of the ceiling.

So, this case wasn't ideal, he thought, trying to console himself. Few had been. He'd been in worse predicaments—maybe not as confusing or frustrating or downright inane, but definitely worse. He'd never forgive George for sticking him in the middle of a three-ring circus, but his debt would be paid. He knew how to be flexible and how to adapt. If the Babbitt woman was unorthodox, he'd handle this case in an unorthodox manner, the bottom line being, he *would* handle it.

He fell asleep fortifying this belief in his mind. He dreamed of Trudy's beguiling face, her smiling lips, her shining eyes . . . his hands around her throat.

Suddenly he awoke to the most ungodly commotion he'd ever heard. Metal clanked and women screamed, and he heard the unmistakable sound of gushing water.

Walker stepped into a pair of well-worn jeans, grabbed his gun, and rushed out into the hallway.

To their mutual astonishment, he came face-to-face with Helena. She let out a high-pitched wail of fright at the sight of his drawn gun; he sucked in an audible gasp of shock at the sight of her, wet from head to toe.

"Put that thing away!" she ordered him, her heavy makeup sagging down her face like melting wax. "This is an emergency!"

"What's happening?" he called out as he watched her move her bulky body down the stairs with remarkable speed. Even before he realized that he wasn't going to get an answer, he was rushing down the hall toward the bathroom and the sounds of a distraught female and surging water.

Trudy was standing in a pool of water near the sink, getting drenched to the bone as she fought to keep her hands capped over the stem of a water faucet handle. She might as well have been trying to hold back Old Faithful. The water pressure was such that it shot up through her fingers and squirted out from under her hands; when she reached out with one hand for a towel, it burst forth like a geyser.

The intrepid Walker attacked the spout without a moment's hesitation. He picked up the pipe wrench on the counter and, disregarding the dousing he was about to get, plunged into the steady stream of cold water to twist the stem back into place, cutting off the water supply. With great forethought he was careful to put the wrench back down on the counter-top before turning to Trudy for an explanation.

"You couldn't have waited until after I'd had my morning coffee to do this?" he asked, making no secret of his exasperation. "Do you always get up this early?"

"I couldn't sleep. I . . ."

"What? What're you staring at?"

"You," she said, a bit stunned, even as her gaze

lowered to reexamine the sweeping expanse of brawny, bare chest and strong, full-muscled shoulders he was displaying without any of the self-consciousness *she* was feeling at that moment. She knew a sense of great regret when she took note of the fact that in his haste Walker had left the top two buttons on his jeans undone and that he didn't appear to have anything on under them.

Having an answer to her night-long mystery and knowing the exact state of his undress during the night did nothing to take the edge off her unrest.

"You need a haircut, Ian," she said, grasping for something to say. "I could trim it for you if you'd like."

"Is that a joke?"

When her smile drooped, and she lowered her gaze from his, he knew she hadn't made her offer in jest and that he'd hurt her feelings. Impulsively he turned, wiped the water off the mirror, and reconsidered the length of his hair. "I don't know. I like it like this. Does it look bad?"

"Well, no. Personally I like a man's hair to be that long-but-not-too-long length. But I always thought you needed to be . . . what is it? . . . cut right and uptight to work for the government. Fred wasn't uptight, but he was cut right, and Mr. Fillmore was both, and they were only bodyguards. But you're not cut right and even though you seem angry most of the time, I don't think you're classically uptight. You're not what I expected a government agent to look like. You really do look more like a mercenary, although you get rather perturbed when people call you that, I've noticed."

Walker narrowed his eyes as he watched her through the mirror, suspicion running rampant in his mind. "It's not going to work, Trudy. Distraction tactics aren't going to get you out of this one. What the hell were you doing in here?"

"The sink was leaking," she said simply. "It almost drove me nuts last night when the two of us were in here. . . . Oh, your eyes look so much better this morning. Not as red. Is your face tender? It's blotchy, but it doesn't look too bad."

"I'm fine," he said, aware for the first time that his eyes still felt dry and scratchy, though not as painful as they had been the night before. "But I didn't know you could method-act plumbing. Is this another one of Roy's helpful ideas?"

"No. And I have to tell you, Ian, that I really don't like it when you're sarcastic. I can't afford a real plumber, but I've recently discovered that I happen to be very good at plumbing. I have a book on it, and when I fixed the leak in the kitchen sink last week, this didn't happen." She paused momentarily. "Of course, I remembered to turn the main water valve off that time. Sometimes I'm a little forgetful."

"Like when you forgot to tell the people living in your house that someone might be trying to kill you?"

"I did tell them," she said, somewhat indignant. "I told them the whole story. And when Mr. Fillmore and Fred came, I told everyone who they were and why they were here. And then we agreed not to talk about it."

"What?"

"I don't like talking about it," she said, feeling defensive. She grabbed a bath towel off the countertop and went down on her hands and knees to begin sopping up the water. "I told them that there was a chance that someone might come looking to kill me, and if that made them uncomfortable, they shouldn't move in here. When they all decided to stay, I asked them not to talk about it because I don't like thinking about it all the time. Okay?"

"No. It's not okay, Trudy. It's something you *need* to think about." He watched as she stood to wring out her towel over the bathtub, and then in a softer voice he asked, "Why wouldn't you enter the witness protection program, Trudy?"

She shifted her weight uneasily under his deep, probing gaze. She wanted him to understand and yet her feelings were so old and vague, it was hard to explain.

"When people run away from what they fear, they run alone. They hide alone. I don't need to have a lot of people around me. I'm content to just be by myself. But I can't stand to be alone. Can you understand that?"

Loneliness was something Walker understood. As a matter of fact, he knew it well enough to accept it as a valid excuse for her actions. He was also beginning to suspect that there might be more in her head than just thin air.

He took another towel off the rack and dropped it into the lake on the bathroom floor. When it was soaked, he picked it up and stood over the tub beside Trudy to wring it out. "Well, I guess time will tell whether you made the right decision or not. And I didn't have any plans for the next few weeks anyway," he said with careful casualness, watching her out of the corner of his eye.

The brilliant smile she offered him tied his stomach in knots, and again he wondered what he'd missed by not kissing her the night before. He'd never kissed a walking catastrophe before, he speculated as he glanced around at the damage she'd caused. Kissing her might well prove to be the experience of a lifetime. Something akin to skydiving without a parachute or wading into piranha-infested waters.

She moved away and began sopping up the water on the vanity. Walker dropped his towel into the puddle again. That was when he caught sight of the bra strap cutting across the middle of her back, outlined by the wet and clinging white T-shirt she wore.

Damn, he muttered to himself. What was the matter with him? Had he become so cold, so inert inside that he'd actually passed up a perfect opportunity to ogle a woman in a wet T-shirt? Had the world become such an ugly place for him, filled with so much treachery and deceit that he could so easily overlook the little pleasures in life? A wild panic seized him. He was suddenly filled with an intense fear. So much so that his hands began to shake.

Walker didn't want to be dead inside. Not anymore. Not ever again. He saw Trudy pick up the wrench and bow her back to wipe under it, exaggerating the strap across her back.

"Trudy?"

"Hmmm?"

Turn around slowly and look at me. The words were on his lips; he wanted to say them. He wanted her to turn and face him, to make his body stir with desire, to make him throb with need, but he just couldn't do it. Not yet.

"What did you do when you worked for Packston?" he asked, retrieving his towel to repeat the clean-up procedure. "He owns a toy company, doesn't he?"

"Yes. I was one of the people in his think tank."

"His what?"

"Well, we called ourselves a think tank, but most of us were graphic designers and engineers who thought up new games and toys and then figured out the cheapest and safest way to make them," she said, setting the wrench down on the edge of the counter again and moving to a new area. "Sometimes Mr. Packston would buy the patent to an idea for a toy and then give it to us, and of course, we had marketing people to help with new trends and things like that. It was a wonderful job. I miss it."

Walker was on his hands and knees, wiping up the water, working at keeping his mind a complete blank and only half listening to Trudy's words.

He'd used women before. Occasionally for a specific purpose, more often for his own gratification. Why not Trudy? He was aching to see Trudy's small, firm breasts under two thin layers of wet cloth, her nipples hard from the chilling water. He just wanted

a look. It wasn't as if he were planning an orgy.
Rita Polanski had bigger boobs than Trudy's. They'd
been huge, pink-tipped orbs of delight to Walker as
a thirteen-year-old. What was the fascination, some
twenty years later, with two baseball-sized mounds
that didn't even qualify as true knockers? Where
was the potential for incredible fantasies there? And
why couldn't he raise his head to sneak a peep?

"Have you ever heard of a game called Beetle
Stompers? Or the Baby See, Baby Do doll? They
were both mine," he heard her say. "And I helped
with the whole line of Mighty Boarbon action fig-
ures. I'll bet your children have a couple of those."

"I don't have any children," he muttered, stunned
by the timing of her question. Why did she have to
bring up the subject of kids now? He knew where
they came from and how they got there. There were
parts of his body that were taking an avid interest
in the conversation and making him extremely
uncomfortable.

"Are you married?"

"No."

Her mind lingered on this briefly. "It's probably
just as well that you aren't," she said. "I know I
wouldn't like being married to you."

"Because you think I'm angry all the time?"

"Oh, that doesn't bother me." She laughed softly.
"But I wouldn't like going to bed alone every night,
wishing you were there beside me and wondering
where you were. I wouldn't enjoy going out to buy
pretty, flimsy little nighties if you were never around
to see them. It wouldn't be any fun to—"

"I get the picture," he interjected gruffly. "Hand
me another towel."

He would have gotten the towel himself, but he
was afraid to stand up, and he didn't dare look at
her. Her words had bypassed his mind and gone
directly to the nerve endings in his body. His fondness for wet T-shirts was all but forgotten, wiped
away by his desire to see her in a pretty, flimsy

nightie, alone in bed, wishing he were there beside her.

She laid a towel on the edge of the counter within his reach and went on talking. "Just think of all the wonderful reunions we'd have, though." She sighed. "After months and months of not seeing each other or being together, you know, sexually?"

"All right already. Could we *please* change the subject now?" he asked, making the mistake of glancing up at her and pulling on the towel at the same time. The fullness and perfect symmetry of her breasts lent power to his tug on the towel.

Pain split through his temple and eyes as the wrench, half hidden under the towel, flipped off the counter and bounced off the side of Walker's face.

At first he thought he'd been struck with lightning for his impure thoughts about Trudy. Then, through a vacuum of pain, he registered the blood on his fingers and the wrench on the floor and knew it hadn't been an act of God, but yet another act of Trudy Babbitt's.

"Dammit to hell, woman. Are you trying to kill me, or what?" he shouted, instinctively turning his back to her, a natural reaction for survival. "No. Don't help me. Go stand up against that wall over there and just . . . just stay out of my way."

"Don't be silly, Ian. You're hurt. Oh my. You're bleeding too. Let me look at it," she said in a calm, authoritative manner—indeed, in the fashion of a person accustomed to seeing people wounded and bleeding, Walker noticed.

"Hell's bells, Trudy," Helena said from the doorway. "You could have told me the water main was under the . . . now what's happened? Is that blood I see?"

"Oh, Helena, Ian's hit himself in the head with the wrench, and he won't let me help him," Trudy said, pulling at Walker's arm in an effort to remove his hands from his face.

"I didn't hit *myself* in the head with a wrench, and I can take care of it. Just get away from me."

"Let her help you, boy," Helena said. "She's good at this sort of thing. She patched that first fella— that first bodyguard—when he fell off the roof. That fool was lucky he didn't break his neck. What was his name again, dear?"

"Mr. Fillmore," Trudy said, still trying to get close enough to Walker to inspect his injury.

"What the hell was he doing on the roof?" Walker asked, peering through his fingers to address Helena.

"No one is too sure about that. But we suspect he was trying to get Trudy off the roof."

"What were *you* doing on the roof?" he asked, turning to squint through his hands at Trudy. She was quick to act on this opportunity, prying both hands away as she told him.

"I'd just gotten a kitten to replace the one that ran away shortly after I moved here. Cats don't like to move, you know."

"The roof. The roof," he prompted her, impatient and tense as she gingerly examined his wound. The pain was considerable, but not enough to keep him from noticing the way her wet T-shirt clung to her upper torso like a second layer of skin.

"Well, the poor little thing had climbed out my bedroom window and onto the roof, and then she wouldn't come back in. So I went out to get her. Come sit over here so I can get a better look at this."

Once again seated on the lid of the commode with Trudy's chest in his face, Walker fought to keep himself distracted. "What happened to Fillmore?"

"Oh, that man," she said, annoyed even in her preoccupation with his wound. "He followed me out onto the roof because he was afraid I'd fall. I told him I wouldn't, but he wouldn't listen to me. And then he tried to take the kitten away from me."

"Because it climbed out on the roof?"

"No. No. He only wanted to carry her inside for

me. But she was frightened, and she knew me better than she knew him."

A cackling sound came from Helena as she stood in the doorway, laughing. "Tell him the rest of the story, Trudy."

"Let me guess," Walker said. "The two of you fought over the cat and Fillmore fell off the roof."

"Yes. It was awful." Trudy dabbed a stinging antiseptic to a shallow, inch-long laceration on Walker's temple. He sucked in air between his teeth. He focused his attention on her lips as she blew on the site of his throbbing pain, a sensation that was rapidly manifesting itself in other parts of his body. "I thought for sure he was dead, or that he'd at least broken his back. Thankfully it wasn't anything worse than a concussion."

"Tell him what Fillmore did. Tell him the worst of it," Helena urged, showing her eagerness to hear the story again.

Trudy looked down into Walker's face, sadness and regret in her eyes. Softly and conclusively she stated, "He killed my cat."

"Fillmore killed your cat?" Walker was astonished and disgusted at once. It wasn't the cat's fault the man fell off the roof. He could understand and sympathize with the man if he'd tried to kill Trudy. But the cat?

Trudy gave him a solemn nod, her bottom lip quivering pathetically.

"He fell on it."

Four

"She's a ditz, George. She's a target for every fluke in the universe. Everything she touches either bleeds or falls apart," Walker told his old friend and evil taskmaster, one of the few people in the world he felt he could confide in.

His pride prevented him from telling George that he suspected Trudy of trying to systematically kill off her protectors and that he'd called him because he'd felt a need to have an ally on the outside. The excuse he *did* use was his need for more information on the house's inhabitants. He'd dealt with left-wing guerrilla terrorists who were less suspicious than his fellow boarders.

"I haven't been here twenty-four hours and already she's slugged me, kicked me, Maced me in the face, and split my head open with a wrench. I hope you're happy," Walker complained.

George laughed. "Have you read her file? There were death threats before the trial. Trudy may be a little klutzy, but she's got a lot of guts."

"There's a big difference between guts and stupidity, you know."

"You ought to know, pal."

"What's that supposed to mean?"

"Think about it," George said, more amused than

61

intimidated by Walker's indignation. Walker never changed, which was one of the many reasons George admired him. He never changed, never gave an inch, and never gave up on anything or anyone. These were good, honorable qualities in any man. But when they were stretched to their limits, battered and abused by time and warped by the world's atrocities, they were dangerous.

Walker continued to list his grievances, but George was lost in thought. His mind had drifted back several days to a time he had hoped he'd never have to see. . . .

"Go to hell, George. I won't do it."

"You will if you want a job here, my friend," George said, his voice revealing little of the empathy he felt for the man who slouched in the chair across from him. He could remember still how emasculating it felt to be yanked in out of the cold.

"Some friend."

The derision in Walker's dark eyes had irritated George. "Damn you, Walker. Don't blame me for this. You brought it on yourself. We have rules, you know. And you've gone out of your way to break them all. I warned you before about this. Repeatedly. It's not my fault that you're too damned bullheaded to listen to anyone."

"I got the job done, didn't I?"

"Damn right. And that's the *only* reason we didn't go ahead and put your butt through the grinder." George got up and, with agitated steps and hand movements, refilled his cup with coffee before turning back to face Walker. "This last stunt of yours put us in a very sticky position. You're lucky you caught that guy, or we'd have left you out there to burn. There are several groups of very unhappy people who would love to see you strung up by your thumbs."

Angrily Walker sat up straighter in the chair. "Well, thanks for bringing me in, man. That was real decent of you. And now this opportunity of a lifetime you're giving me, to baby-sit this looney-tune cousin of yours. . . . Hell, George, I can't begin to tell you how much I appreciate it," he said, his sarcasm stinging. "Why the hell don't you just let 'em blow my brains out? Or are you planning to enjoy watching me die a slow death by boredom?"

George closed his eyes and gave a resigned sigh. Walker was too angry to listen to reason. Not that he held that against the man. He was his friend. And he did understand what he was going through. For the past twelve years I. N. Walker had been one of the agency's best kept secrets. A federal agent in the underground who, through any means possible, ferreted out terrorists, smuggled information, thwarted uprisings, and in general lived on the brink of disaster. Every atom of his body was part of a finely tuned machine. He could sense danger days before it happened and miles before it got to him. He could kill with a flick of his wrist. He knew more about espionage, the underground, and world affairs than any other agent. But something was wrong.

Walker had always been daring and seemingly fearless. But over the past few years he'd also gotten . . . out of control. He took needless risks. Made and carried out bold, life-threatening choices. It was almost as if Walker saw himself as indestructible. He was like a star going nova. He was burning out.

For his own good and the nation's welfare, they had decided to pull him out of the field. If not permanently, at least until his latest escapade had blown over. He was far too valuable to lose simply because he refused to cover his own tail and follow the rules. Maybe some rest and a little humiliation would do him some good.

George opened his eyes and gave his angry, resentful friend a calculated stare. Finally he said, "You are relieved of any further field work as of this moment and until such time as I feel you are physically and emotionally fit to resume your duties." He paused to let this sink into Walker's head. "In the interim, these are your choices as I see them, Walker. The first is an official suspension. The second is a nice quiet little desk job in Minnesota, where you'll be buried under so much paper that no one outside this office will even know you're still alive." A pregnant pause. "Or, there are those little favors you owe me for saving your skin in Beirut a few years ago, and then again in Cairo in eighty-three, not to mention Costa Rica and Bogota."

George took Walker's fierce glare in stride while he flicked his Bic to one end of a fat cigar, and then he continued.

"And seeing as how we're such good friends and all, I'd be willing to wrap all of those trifling incidents into this one little personal favor I have to ask of you."

"That's it? Those are the only choices I have—as you see them?" Walker asked, his temper only barely contained.

"Well, there is one more," George said, knowing sympathy and compassion would only make Walker more belligerent. "You can always pick up your marbles and go play somewhere else."

"Don't tempt me, George," Walker said after a long deadly silence. And then he'd stood to pick up the sheet of paper that listed both Trudy's and Madge and Henry Babbitt's addresses and left the room.

George had sighed with relief, glad to have Walker safely stowed away until more satisfactory arrangements could be made for him and not the least bit worried that Walker would ever decide to play games with someone else, because he knew Walker. Walker never changed, never gave an inch, and never gave up on anything or anyone. . . .

"Dammit, George, are you listening to me?"

"You bet, buddy, and I feel for you. I really do. What's she doing now?" he asked, amusement stretching his grin wider.

"I told you. She's cooking dinner. I'll bet she

knows the entire fire department on a first-name basis."

"Give her a break, Walker. She's had a rough time of it."

"There's a good reason for that, most likely," he said, a bit cryptic as he recalled his talk with Trudy the night before. And then more to himself than to Phillips he said, "It oughtta be interesting to see what it is."

"Hang in there, man. I'll make a few calls regarding your roommates and the neighbors on both sides of the street. I've got a friend in the Justice Department, so I can get the general lay of the land with Packston too. I'll get back to you as soon as I can."

"Thanks, George," Walker said, feeling not quite so alone anymore. "And George?"

"Yeah."

"You do know that I don't want to go to Arlington if anything happens to me, don't you? Send whatever's left of me to my sister in Michigan. She'll see to the rest."

"It is now six P.M.," the talking clock in the dining room announced as five of the residents gathered for dinner. It was apparently part of Roy's routine to sleep most of the day and arise late in the evening to go to work.

And so it was Ruby, the vamp; Walker; the shy, seductive, and secretive Charlotte; Trudy; and the intensely ugly and formidable Helena who came together that evening. The four sat mesmerized in disbelief while Trudy served the night's fare.

"This is something new that the cute little Hungarian lady at the market told me about. She had a name for it, but for the life of me, I can't remember what it is," Trudy was saying as she set a large platter of what might loosely be termed as food in the center of the table.

Contrary to what everyone at the agency thought, Walker was not suicidal. He didn't want to die, and yet he would have bet his life that what Trudy had every intention of feeding them was raw liver. It was partially covered in some sort of tomato sauce and artistically arranged on a bed of overcooked noodles, but the truth of the matter couldn't be disguised. It *was* uncooked liver.

He stared at it long and hard, afraid to look up at the expression on the others' faces. If they were gleeful and salivating, he'd buy silver bullets for his gun.

"Be careful of these rolls now, they're hot from the oven," Trudy said, coming back into the room from the kitchen and setting a small basket of golden, aromatic rolls on the table. Beside it she placed a bowl of brussels sprouts, not a favorite of Walker's but something he felt safe in eating.

"I do believe you've outdone yourself, Trudy," Helena said in a dispassionate tone of voice as she picked up the platter of slimy red meat and took her share before passing it on. "Your meals are always such an adventure."

"Mmmm," Charlotte agreed, taking the plate from her mother. Her face was a mask of nonexpression.

"We had Russian meat loaf last week, Mr. Walker," Ruby said. She looked at the slim gold watch on her wrist before making eye contact with him. "Siberians have nothing over Trudy's cooking. It was as good as being there."

Walker's brows shot up as he felt a sudden and forceful undercurrent in the table conversation. He saw a definite warning and threat in Ruby's eyes as she passed the platter to him after taking her portion.

Walker's piece of extremely rare meat slithered onto his plate, followed by an ample supply of noodles and pasty red sauce. Once again he glanced at the faces around the table. Helena had her eyes trained on the talking clock as she buttered her roll over and over again. Charlotte was cutting a brus-

sels sprout into tiny little pieces and eating them
heartily. Ruby popped her vegetables into her mouth
whole and once again checked the time on her
watch. But no one was touching the meat.

"I love trying out new recipes," Trudy said,
addressing Walker. "I grew up on meat and pota-
toes, which was okay." She shrugged. "My granny
didn't believe in doing things fancy or experiment-
ing or trying anything new. But I like a new experience once in a while, don't you, Ian?"

"Oh, yeah." He'd once spent four hours in a snake
pit before being rescued by a band of loyalist parti-
sans, who'd handcuffed him to a jeep and held a
rifle to his ribs for several more hours until his identity could be confirmed. That was an experience.
And yet, at the moment, it paled in the face of having to eat raw liver.

They all jumped when the phone rang, but no one
got up to answer it. Their gazes met and then slid
in Trudy's direction as they sat waiting for her to
get up and answer it.

She had a forkful of meat cut and ready to eat
when she looked up to find them all staring at her.

"Oh. I forgot. It's my night to answer the phone
too," she said, laying her fork down and leaving the
table to do just that.

"Abracadabra," Helena said, producing a sixth
plate from somewhere under the table. "Quick.
Hurry."

She flipped her liver and most of her brussels
sprouts onto the plate, then held it for Charlotte
while she did the same.

"Get it all now," Helena said, motioning with her
head to the serving platter, where two or three more
pieces remained. "That cold Russian meat loaf sandwich she made me last Saturday damn near killed
me."

Walker didn't hesitate when it came his turn to
dispose of his meal.

"Mother, do you think she forgot to turn the oven on again?" Charlotte asked in a low voice.

"Who knows. With liver it doesn't make much of a difference, does it?"

They all pretty much agreed that it didn't.

"Don't forget your roll," Ruby said, tapping hers on the table as if it were a little round rock. "They're very deceptive."

"What are you going to do with it?" Walker asked, having already drawn his own conclusions. It seemed odd to him that such a strange group of people would go to so much trouble to save Trudy's feelings, but he knew he didn't have the time to give it much thought. He joined in eagerly, more to get out of eating the meal than for any other reason, and let the spirit sweep him away.

He looked over at the plate next to his. He grimaced and then tossed Trudy's meat onto the plate beside his own.

"I'll say I ate it," he told the others. When he looked at them, they were smiling their approval at him. He cleared his throat self-consciously and asked again, "What are you going to do with it now?"

"Chowder loves Friday nights," Helena said. She winked at him.

A few minutes later they were all leaning back in their chairs, looking entirely full and satisfied when Trudy returned to the table. "I don't know why Horace picks this particular time to call every week. He must have a schedule or something for calling his friends and checking up on them, because it never fails, every Friday night at ten minutes after six, the phone rings, and it's Horace."

"Who's Horace?" It wasn't merely a professional question. Walker wanted to be able to thank the man if he ever met him.

"Horace Turner. He's our sheriff," she said, frowning at her plate as if she couldn't figure out what was wrong with it. "He's a very sweet old gentleman.

He calls to check up on us and see how we're doing. Did someone eat my dinner for me?"

"I did," Walker said, feeling extremely foolish. It was one thing to think she was crazy, but something else to have her thinking the same thing about him. "I'm sorry. I couldn't help myself."

"Well, I'm glad you liked it," she said, greatly pleased as she stood to clear away her dishes and the remains of the dinner. "Fred was a very good eater too. I like that in a man. I really do."

Walker stood on the front porch with his hands in his rear pockets. He took deep gulps of air and tried to ignore the gnawing hunger pains in his belly. Trudy, he'd noticed, had slipped into the kitchen for a bowl of cereal earlier in the evening, but in order to keep up the pretext that he'd consumed her meal with great relish, he'd gone hungry.

He shook his head and quirked his lips into a half-smile. What a strange lot they were, Trudy and her boarders. He began to question the need for further background investigations on them now that it was so clear to him the lengths they'd go simply to spare her feelings. If any one of them were trying to kill her, they would have let her eat her own cooking by now.

He'd seen this phenomenon before in small, close-knit groups. There always seemed to be one special person among them who for one reason or another they silently, unconsciously, and unanimously felt they needed to protect. It was very apparent to Walker that the boarders felt this way about Trudy. They all seemed to have plenty of problems of their own, and yet they were intent on making Trudy's problems theirs as well.

However, this wasn't an indication that Walker could trust any of them. He'd learned his lessons about trust as a rookie. He didn't even trust Trudy to keep *herself* out of harm's way, much less the collection of kooks and misfits she'd surrounded herself with.

His stomach growled loudly as he watched a county sheriff's car drive by the house. It slowed, picked up some speed, and then parked down the road, several houses away. No one got out. For long moments he observed the car, his uneasiness increasing with each second. Turning his head, he glanced through the open window to make sure that Trudy was still lounging on the couch in the living room, reading, before giving in to his urge to satisfy his curiosity about the patrol car.

He stepped down off the porch and slowly made his way along the walk. He'd reached the curb when the driver of the car got out and started walking back in Walker's direction.

"You're the new one, eh?" a uniformed man in his sixties said, his voice a gravely, grating noise in the dark. His gray-white hair shone in the moonlight, and he walked with a distinct limp. "I see Compton didn't waste any time gettin' outta here once he got the word, eh? This is for you."

He held a white paper bag out to Walker. His rotund abdomen and slow, lazy gait left Walker with the impression that in a chase, the man would be of little use. And yet there was something about him that commanded a certain amount of respect and fear. The way he spoke or the way he held himself; something indefinable told him the man was someone to be reckoned with.

"What is it?" he asked.

"Dinner. The others'll find a way to get some food, but you boys are sorta stuck, watchin' Trudy. Compton damn near starved to death the first coupla Friday nights he was here, till we fell on this plan." He let Walker take the bag from his hands and peek into it. "Wanna walk the perimeter?"

"You're Horace Turner?" The man confirmed it with a nod. "Marines?" Walker asked, sensing the man's military training, recognizing certain gestures and postures by reflex.

He opened the bag, took out a paper-wrapped hamburger, and began to eat as they walked, moving toward the rear of Trudy's house.

"Twenty-two years. Coulda had my own desk after I caught this in 'Nam"—he gestured to his leg—"but I sorta lost my taste for it, ya know? Been the M.P. around here ever since."

"How closely are you involved in this assignment?" There hadn't been any mention in Compton's report of local support.

"Mostly, I just bring food on Friday nights. I been savin' 'em all from food poisoning since I picked that Roy fella up on a morals offense when he first moved here. My callin' every Friday night was his idea. Sorta surprised she hasn't caught on to it yet."

"A morals offense?"

"A misunderstanding, really. 'Course, I met Trudy a little later when she rear-ended me at the stoplight downtown. Right off, I knew there was somethin' different about her. Never once said she was sorry for hittin' me, you know." Walker couldn't speak with his mouth full, so he nodded, and Turner continued.

"Invited me to dinner instead. Roy fed my dinner to the dog, and I been indebted to him ever since. Mostly, I'm just worried about Trudy and around if ya need me."

Again Walker nodded his understanding. "Where's Flint Mountain from here?" he asked, knowing his time was limited and that a discussion about Trudy's cooking could only give him indigestion.

"Not far. Not even a mountain really. It's a campground about thirty miles east of here. She still plannin' on taking her Sunshine girls out there next month?"

"Yeah. She's set on it," he said, resigned but confident in his tracking and surveillance skills. "She's making a dry run tomorrow and says that if I'm going to insist on going with her, that I'll have to stay out of sight so she can pretend to be alone. How hard could it be to track one woman?"

"Or a herd of 'em for that matter, eh?" Both men laughed. "Won't be hard at all, considering where you're going. It's a controlled area. Nothing out of the ordinary. But I'd be glad to help out if you need me."

"Thanks. I might take a two-way with me just in case, if you've got one." He still felt uneasy about having no backup and no means of communication, no matter how innocent the outing seemed. He knew that nothing was ever as innocent as it appeared . . . except maybe Trudy.

He thought about her inside the house, stretched out on the couch, her nose stuck in a science-fiction paperback. She wasn't a total innocent. It didn't take a man of the world to know that her body wasn't inexperienced. And there was an awareness in her eyes that led him to believe that she wasn't unfamiliar with the effect she had on him. In fact, there had been several times throughout the day when he had caught her watching him, a look of lust in her eyes that outmatched any Ruby could have come up with.

No. Trudy wasn't innocent in that way. Her purity was deeper, more basic to her personality. Intuitively he knew that her heart had been broken; she'd been disappointed and touched by pain like so many other people in the world . . . like himself. And still she trusted; she was optimistic and fault-blind to those around her. She was innocent in a childlike way in her heart.

There was a sudden aching pressure in Walker's chest that forced Trudy from his mind and brought his attention back to Horace Turner.

"I want to know about any strangers you see in town. I don't care if they're just stopping for gas. I want them checked out," he said more forcefully than he had intended. He felt an acute, almost animallike protectiveness surge through him.

"You got it. Leave your car unlocked tonight, and I'll put a two-way under the front seat." Turner paused, rocking back and forth on his feet. "I see the girl didn't waste much time puttin' her mark on ya."

Walker frowned in confusion, and the old marine laughed, motioning to the bandage on his temple. Automatically his fingers touched the dressing, and despite the anger he'd felt earlier, he chuckled. "She sure did. Never once said she was sorry, either."

They laughed together and passed generalities until Walker finished his meal, and then they parted on favorable terms.

Walker's breath quickened automatically when he walked into the living room several minutes later to find Trudy dressed in a short pink satin robe, waiting to bid him good night. He experienced a sinking, defeated feeling in the pit of his stomach. That she couldn't cook worth beans didn't seem to carry much weight with his libido. Despite all her faults and idiosyncrasies, it was all too clear to him that she had no problems filling a flimsy little robe to perfection.

"Oh, there you are," Trudy said, standing and smoothing the robe down around her waist, nervously pulling the sash just a little tighter.

It looked like an entirely natural adjustment to make to one's clothing when rising from a sitting position. It also had an entirely natural effect on Walker, considering the growing attraction he had for her.

"I wasn't sure if we were supposed to go to bed together or not, so I waited up for you."

"What?" His joints went suddenly weak and spastic.

"Well, Fred used to check my room and lock the window before he'd let me in to go to sleep, but if you'd rather sneak in later *after* I've gone to sleep, like you did last night, that's okay too. Mr. Fillmore did it both ways, but he was a nervous sort of person. I was just wondering which you preferred."

For a change, her explanation was logical, but it did little to lessen the rate of his heartbeat or release the tension in his body. Every nerve synapse inside him went on red alert as his gaze followed the shiny lines of the robe over the curves of her breasts and her slender waist and hips. Her legs were smooth, and the short robe seemed to accentuate their length. He dug his nails into the palms of his hands until pain registered in his mind.

"I'll go up with you now. I'll also check on you during the night when I feel it's necessary, okay?" he said, his tone terse, his words more harsh than he'd meant them to be.

Trudy arched a brow to acknowledge his unwarranted ill humor. How did she always seem to make him angry? she wondered. What was she doing wrong? She would have given anything to be able to get past his anger, to soothe and heal whatever was causing it.

"Fine," she said softly, refusing to give in to his distemper.

He followed her up the stairs and down the hall to her room. He might have felt some shame for his behavior if he weren't so irritated by the way her hips swayed when she walked.

Mentally reviewing all the reasons he had for keeping his hands off of her was becoming less and less effective. Control was something he knew. He was a master at controlling himself and manipulating those around him. It was irksome that Trudy and the feelings he had for her weren't complying with the facts.

She stood silently in the hall while he secured her bedroom for the night. He could feel her watching his every move.

"You make me feel very safe, Ian," she said impulsively, struck by the contrast of seeing such a dark, sinister-looking man standing amid the bright, innocuous shapes of the toys and dolls in her room. And yet it was his fierce appearance that allowed everything around him to look innocent and harmless.

He turned toward her. She looked small and vulnerable and incredibly sexy. It occurred to him that were his mother alive, she would have liked Trudy. He thought of Clinker, a golden retriever he'd grown up with and loved more than anything. He had a sudden mental impression of being warm and secure and waiting for Santa Claus to come.

He was frowning when his eyes focused on Trudy again. Where were all these old memories and feelings coming from? They were beginning to give him the creeps.

"Yeah, well, you probably don't have too much to worry about unless Packston gets a new trial. If he were going to kill you for revenge, he'd have done it by now," he said, hoping to ease her mind.

She smiled, "Mr. Packston isn't the only danger in the world."

He nodded, feeling awkward and at a loss for words. He liked knowing that she thought he could protect her from the whole world. He knew at that moment that he would do exactly that if the need arose. He wanted to. He wanted her to always feel safe.

"Are . . . are these the toys you worked on?" he asked, motioning generally at the playthings in the room. More now than before he knew how much the room suited her—absolutely feminine with childlike accents.

"Yes. Some of them. Most are prototypes that didn't pan out."

"One-of-a-kind originals, huh?" he said, looking at a tall, thin doll in a pink tutu. A one-of-a-kind original—like Trudy.

He turned on a mechanical turtle and watched it pop its head and feet in and out of its shell before it spun around and rolled away. It was about to fall off the shelf, when Trudy reached out to catch it.

She stood within easy touching distance. Could she tell how much he wanted to put his hands on her body? he wondered. What would she do if he kissed her?

They stared at each other for a long moment before their unbidden attraction became too strenuous, causing them to look away.

"Would you like to talk, Ian?"

"About what?"

"Anything. Your job. Life. I'm a very good listener, believe it or not."

There was an openness in her expression, an eagerness to understand whatever he chose to tell her. There was also sympathy and kindness, both of which annoyed him unreasonably.

"My job is to baby-sit you, whether I want to or not, and *that* is life," he said. He walked to the door without giving her a second glance. He would have kept on going if she hadn't spoken.

"I wish I'd known you before you became so angry at everyone."

He turned to look at her, his eyes narrow and glaring. "What makes you think I'm angry at everyone? How do you know it isn't just you I'm angry at?"

"Because I think you *like* me."

Trudy was so surprised when he grabbed her up into his arms and clamped his mouth over hers that she forgot to take note of the sizzles and sparks that she normally encountered with a first kiss. As a matter of fact, she wasn't taking note of anything. It was as if her arms and her legs no longer existed. She felt as if she'd been sucked up into a vacuum. Her body burned as something hot and molten surrounded her. A distant rumbling came from deep within her. Her world churned like the inside of an active volcano, full of fire and might. Rising on a force only the gods could generate and control, greater than any human had known before, she rose to the top of the mountain. She was prepared to be jettisoned in a massive explosion, spewed out into the universe as so many pieces of dust. . . .

Suddenly Ian pulled back. His chest rose and fell as if he'd just run a great distance. His hands shook violently as they held her an arm's length away. The passion in his eyes terrified Trudy, increasing the weakness in her knees.

He stared at her long and hard, struggling with emotions he'd never dealt with before—animal urges, instinctive drives, impulses beyond his control. He floundered in confusion, felt a desire to cry like a baby, and drew on his pride to keep him alive.

"You're right, Trudy," he said, his voice embarrassingly tight and raspy. "But I like you just a little bit."

Five

"Wow," Trudy whispered in the darkness with a capricious sigh. She had been kissed before, but never like Ian had kissed her. She lay in bed in a stupor, mesmerized by the touch of his lips, wondering how it was that she'd come to miss such an experience before in her life. Falling in love was something she did easily and exceptionally well. How was it that it had never felt like this before?

She had always taken great pleasure in the tingling sensations that zinged through her body and the warm, twisting occurrences deep in her abdomen. She had delighted in the anticipation and knew of no other feelings as enlivening as that sudden lifting in her chest, the way her heart raced and her muscles quickened when she thought of the man who'd most recently enthralled her.

More often than not, however, she chose not to act on her feelings, because of the men who caught her attention. She'd fallen into deep lust with Alex McArthur and Tom Cruise several times each, and the man on the six o'clock news was a daily affair. Handsome strangers in restaurants, charming men in the park, and intriguing characters in books all had the same glorious effect on her.

Ian had that effect on her, but it was different

when he touched her. His hands didn't merely slide over her skin, leaving a trail of goose flesh in their wake. They gripped the essence of who she was, wrenched at her heart, and aroused a hunger in her body that gnawed and ached to be satisfied.

Infatuation and falling in love were not new to Trudy, but her feelings for Ian were.

He had stormed off in a huff, muttering things about dizzy females and inflated egos, but she hadn't missed the way he'd been watching her all day or the amount of self-control he had used in his dealings with her. Nor could she ignore the twinkling in his eyes while he fought to keep an expression of stern disapproval on his face when she spoke to him. Or the difficulty he had breathing, the muscle tremors and the excessive swallowing he did whenever she was close to him. All the signs were there; she knew them by heart. There wasn't a doubt in her mind that they were mutually attracted.

But what now? she wondered, rolling over in bed, hoping to find a comfortable position. Ian wasn't solely someone whose company she enjoyed and who made her feel giddy, light-headed, and tingly all over. He was also an extremely complex man full of secrets and anger and experiences that she knew nothing about. The magnitude of his passions, the power and strength of his spirit, had threatened to consume her. It frightened her. It was like playing with fire. Yet intuitively she trusted him. She sensed that somewhere in Ian was a treasure she'd been searching for all her life. The answers to most of her questions were buried in his heart, but she didn't have the vaguest idea of how to get to them.

And what about Ian? Was he aware of the dynamic dimensions of whatever it was that was drawing them together? What if Ian had become so irrevocably embittered toward the world that he'd forgotten how to love and what it was like to be loved? What had he been doing before he came to watch over her? What could have made him so angry? What could have hurt him that badly?

What if his resentment was so deep that he didn't know it was there? Then wouldn't she owe it to him, as another human being, as someone who had a vested interest in him and who cared about him, to show him that the world wasn't all bad? Didn't the laws of common decency dictate that she soothe him and help to heal his emotional wounds?

Trudy grinned and snuggled deeper into her covers, well pleased with her reasoning.

Granted, her rationale might seem a little self-serving to some people, Trudy contemplated as the night wore on. Allowing oneself to fall in love with someone for their good, when one was bound to fall in love with that person anyway, was not a great humanitarian sacrifice. She wasn't fooling herself. She knew that her heart was set on falling in love with Ian, no matter what her mind advised. And she wasn't for a moment forgetting the fact that once his debt to George was paid, he'd be moving on, and she wouldn't be going with him.

But her heart didn't care about any of that. It had no concept of time as it related to the future. It harbored very few regrets, many sweet memories, and a propensity for giving. It thrived in the here and now. It quickened to Ian's every touch, his slightest glance. It reached out to the pain in him and accepted his anger. It longed to thaw his frosty facade and to bask in his warm, gentle arms.

There were things deep inside Ian that beckoned to her, cried out to her, and she couldn't help but respond to them.

And so she found the notion that *Ian* needed to fall in love extremely consoling when her eyes closed sleepily on the world. She'd continue to fall in love with Ian, and she'd teach him how to love her in return. And when it was over, she wouldn't regret it, because she wouldn't have been able to stop herself anyway, and Ian would know that there were still many good things left in the world.

Believing that all was fair in love and war, she arose the next morning looking forward to seeing Ian again. War first, love later, she decided as she shuffled down the hall to the bathroom.

She took an extra-long shower, knowing her next one wouldn't come until she returned home from her camping trip. She washed her hair twice for the same reason.

"It's about time," Ian growled when she opened the bathroom door and found him standing impatiently in the hall. "Two more seconds and I was coming in to see if you'd slipped and split your head open in the tub."

"Oh, Ian, you worry too much. I put those little rubber daisies on the bottom of the bathtub to prevent that." She went on to explain exactly what had taken her so long and was surprised when he simply stood staring at her.

"Listen to me," she said, feeling foolish. "You probably know a lot more about camping and surviving in the wilderness than I do."

"Flint Mountain is thirty miles from here. That's not exactly wilderness."

"If there's no bathroom, no phone, no electricity, no hot water, and you sleep in a bag on the dirt, it's wilderness. Are you sure you have everything you need? I think you should reconsider Ruby's offer to borrow Roy's electric underwear."

"I don't need any electric underwear." He sighed and slumped against the wall, looking very tired all of a sudden. "Why do I have the feeling that this is going to be the worst twenty-four hours of my life?" he asked.

"I don't know, Ian. I'm beginning to feel better and better about it all the time," she said, bouncing with enthusiasm as she walked into her room and closed the door.

"Swell."

Dressed in her khaki walking shorts, her Sunshine girl T-shirt, knee socks, and sturdy sneakers, Trudy set out toward Flint Mountain without the slightest delay. Through her rearview mirror she watched as Ian steered his car away from the house and followed her through town. When he pulled up behind her at a stop sign, he looked so bored and out of sorts that she couldn't help but laugh, feeling not the slightest bit sorry for him as she did so.

At the campground she saw where he parked the dark blue sedan he'd been driving, but, true to his word, her bodyguard was nowhere to be seen.

Loaded down with a sleeping bag, tent, and what seemed like half a ton of camping gear, she took the Squirrel Trail—an easy hike according to the brochure.

For two hours she went up and down hills, over rocks, across a wide stream, and along a narrow path on the side of a cliff, all bearing the little squirrel signs marking the trail.

By the time she reached the campsite, Trudy had vowed that if she ever got home again, she would sue whoever wrote the brochure for false advertising. The only thing that had kept her from turning around and going back was knowing that Ian was watching and that he would keep her safe.

She took vague notice of the other campers and a group of Sunshine girls before she threw her rolled-up sleeping bag on the ground and flopped down beside it to rest. By the time she had regained her breath and opened her eyes, there were five little girls in Sunshine T-shirts staring at her in open concern.

"Oh my," she said, exaggerating her shame. "I

suppose a real Sunshine girl would never get tuckered out this quickly, would she?"

"No," a freckle-faced girl with red braids said quite plainly. "Where are your girls?" she asked, obviously thinking the worst of Trudy, like perhaps she'd lost them on the trail somewhere.

"Oh, I didn't bring them with me today. You see, I'm not a very good camper, so I thought I'd come up here and get some practice at it before our real campout." She looked at each of the girls in turn. She usually found honesty to be a good policy when dealing with children, so she added, "Actually this is my first time camping. You girls probably know more about it than I do. If you see me doing something really stupid, will you let me know? I don't want to look like an idiot when I bring my girls up."

The girls smiled and nodded and lost much of the skepticism in their facial expressions.

"Are you Trudy Babbitt?" another little girl asked, a frown creasing her young, sun-reddened face.

"Yes." Trudy was thrown off guard. "How did you know that?"

"There was a man in the bushes over there," a third girl said, pointing toward a stand of trees that separated the carefully cleared camping area from a stream of water about a hundred yards away. She bent then, to scratch a bug bite on her leg. "He told us to tell Trudy Babbitt to get off her duff and set up camp before it got dark."

"He said he didn't care if you stumbled around in the dark all night, he wasn't going to do it for you," a little girl with big blue eyes added, her hands on her hips to stress the man's point.

"Is the man a friend of yours?" the first girl asked. "He doesn't seem very nice."

"He's not," Trudy said, perturbed. Ian was supposed to stay out of sight. And then, in a voice she hoped Ian could hear, she added, "You all know about talking to strange men in bushes, don't you? You mustn't ever talk to anyone you don't know. Right?"

"We didn't talk to him," said the blue-eyed girl emphatically. "He talked to us."

"And then he was gone," said another. She snapped her fingers. "Just like that."

"Just like that, huh?" She looked amazed. And again, speaking too loud and lacing her voice with a threatening quality, she said, "Well, he's probably long gone by now, but if you see him again, you run and come tell me. He might be a forest ranger who can identify *every single one* of these trees for us. Wouldn't that be great?"

Without any further help from the girls or the bush man, Trudy began to set up camp. Thinking that it might be a good idea to situate herself so that she could watch the other Sunshine leader in action, she chose a spot within hearing distance and unrolled her tent.

Remarkably camping in the wilderness didn't seem any harder than camping in her backyard. She still wasn't too thrilled with the sport, but it wasn't intolerable. And by the time she'd gathered her wood and started a small fire in her pit, the leader of the Sunshine girls had found the time to come over to introduce herself and invite Trudy to join them for dinner. Trudy was delighted.

Campfire cooking was a requirement for a badge the girls were working on in their group, so Trudy and the leader were excluded from the actual preparation other than making sure that the girls didn't set the woods on fire in the process. The girls' mothers had sent premeasured portions of all the fixings necessary to make "Squatter's Stew" which was very much like vegetable-beef soup. Trudy kept careful notes on the whole procedure.

And, of course, there was the traditional roasted-marshmallow dessert, just as Roy had predicted. They even went so far as to squish the stuff between two graham crackers along with a candy bar. The concoctions made Trudy's teeth itch.

Later, after they'd gathered more wood for the fire

and put away all the food—except for two bags of chips, a box of cheese crackers, and a tin container of oatmeal cookies with extra raisins—the girls sat huddled together around the fire telling the most gruesome, horrifying stories Trudy had ever heard.

Several times, as the shadows disappeared into darkness and the night took on an eeriness that the stories didn't help to dispel, it occurred to her to wonder where Ian had hidden himself. What had he brought with him to eat? Would he be warm enough during the night without Roy's electric underwear?

Frankly the idea of battery-heated longjohns was beginning to appeal to her. It was growing colder, and a dampness had seeped into her bones, even through the jeans and parka she'd changed into earlier.

The girls, the leader, and Trudy all giggled hysterically and tried to scare one another to death as they made one last visit to the bushes for the night. And then, like a mother duck, the leader ushered the girls back to their tents, leaving Trudy and bidding her a fond good-night at her campsite.

Moments later they were all back at Trudy's tent.

"Have you seen Madeline?" the woman asked, distraught, as she squinted her eyes, focusing on the bushes.

"No. I haven't," Trudy said. "But I'll help look for her."

"This isn't funny," the leader said when Freddy Kreuger's name was mentioned in the ranks. "What if it's not a trick? What if she's lost?"

"We didn't go that far. How could she be lost?" one of the girls asked. It was soon apparent that the girls wanted to believe that Madeline was merely playing, but the fear in their eyes told Trudy that they were picking up on the fear and panic in their leader.

"You might be right," she said to the group as a whole. "Why don't you all go ahead and get ready for bed, and let me take a look around, just in case."

The woman smiled her gratitude and hustled the girls back to their campsite while Trudy went back into the underbrush, calling and looking high and low for the naughty little prankster.

With the name Freddy Kreuger still fresh in her mind, her heart stopped and she nearly died of fright when she found a pair of white running shoes attached to a rather long set of denim-clad legs planted at the foot of a large oak tree.

"Oh, Ian! You scared me to death," she scolded him in a harsh whisper, her hand on her chest to calm her heart. "You really shouldn't sneak up on a person like that."

"I owed you one," he said, and then he grinned.

At that moment Trudy forgot all about Madeline. Ian stood facing one of the campfires, its pale light illuminating his face and showing Trudy the most natural, candid expression she'd ever seen him exhibit. For the first time since they'd met, he looked relaxed, friendly, and completely accessible. A thousand questions leapt to her mind. She felt an urgency to ask him everything she'd wondered about him, before the openness in his features vanished again.

"You're enjoying this campout, aren't you." It was a statement rather than a question, but it was just too amazing to let it go unmentioned.

He shrugged and looked embarrassed. "Those stories reminded me of when I was a kid."

"They were awful." She shuddered. "What kind of childhood did you have?"

"No. No." He chuckled. "I meant, sitting around a fire, telling stories like that. I don't remember them being quite so bloodthirsty, though."

"Were you a happy little boy?"

"Of course." He looked confused for a moment, and then he stared at her so intensely that she thought perhaps he might be looking through her, beyond her flesh and blood to the central nature of who she was. He didn't seem to believe what he saw at first, and then, as if he were testing a newly frozen layer of ice on a pond, he said, "Trudy. I'm not . . ." His courage failed him, and the moment was gone. "Forget it. Have you seen the sky lately?"

"No. I was looking for Madeline." She gasped as she remembered. "Have you seen her?"

He grabbed her arm as she stepped away to continue her search, whether he'd seen her or not.

"Shhh . . ." he said. "Wait a second."

"We can talk later, Ian. I . . ."

"Shhh. Wait. She went down to the stream. She's okay. She'll be right back."

"But what if something happens to her? What if she falls in?"

"If she falls in, she'll come back wet. It's only eighteen inches deep. She . . . had an accident, I think, and could use a little privacy right now. She'll be . . ." He turned his head to listen, and then smiled at Trudy. "She's on her way back," he whispered as he pulled her to the dark side of the tree and tugged her into a squatting position.

It was several more seconds before Trudy heard the footsteps and the twigs cracking and breaking as the little girl ran up the path.

"She's frightened," she said, sensing the girl's fear as she ran past them. Her back almost snapped in two when she tried to stand and Ian yanked her back down beside him.

"You'd be scared, too, if you thought Freddy Kreuger was roaming these woods. But that's one brave little girl," he said.

Trudy's imagination hadn't as yet eliminated the possibility of a Freddy-like creature in the woods, though she'd never admit to it. She did, however, covet the admiration in his voice.

"She risked her life to save her dignity," he said softly, close to Trudy's ear. Awe deepened his voice, making it extremely sensual. "I think she scraped one of her knees when she fell. And she went all the way down there alone to clean up, so her friends wouldn't see her crying, even though she wasn't positive that it was a safe thing to do." He paused.

"It's probably not the wisest way to think, but it took a lot of guts just the same." Again he hesitated. "Don't let them make a big deal of it, Trudy. It would humiliate her."

He spoke as if a little humiliation were a fate worse than death, which in this case it could have been, Trudy thought, still a little shaken by the girl's disappearance. But now that she knew the girl was safe, her curiosity was piqued by Ian's reaction.

"What should I say? The girls shouldn't wander off whenever they feel like it."

He turned his head to look at her. She couldn't see the expression on his face, but she could feel his warm breath against her cheek and knew that his lips couldn't be too far away. Her heart began to race, her body shivered from the inside out, and she relished the feeling, anticipated more.

"I don't know all that much about kids, but I think I'd just tell her that you were glad she was back and then make a general announcement not to leave camp without permission."

It was Trudy's turn to marvel in astonishment. Although she had always suspected there was another side to Ian that was kind, understanding, and compassionate, seeing it for the first time had a very strange effect on her.

She felt privileged and trusted. By showing her his private side, it was as if he were making her privy to his secrets and thereby putting her in a position to betray or protect him as she chose. No one had ever given her that much responsibility before.

Because of her size, most people felt as if they needed to protect her, inadvertently making her feel weak and useless. Because of the unexpected turns and twists in the paths she chose to travel, they had a tendency to think of her as someone who couldn't control her own life, a flake, or as Ian himself called her, a ditz—unreliable, untrustworthy, and uncommonly fainthearted. In reality, she was none of those things, except short.

She'd never felt a need to prove herself to those people. She had shown her strength to herself over and over again. Testifying against Mr. Packston had taken more courage and strength than she'd ever realized she'd had. But she didn't do it to impress anyone. She had testified because she was simply an honest and dutiful person.

Only her friends, people who had taken the time to truly know her, knew of her strength and character. That Ian would share his vulnerability with her, that he would look on her as an equal, if only for a brief time, meant more to her than anything else she could remember.

When she didn't answer right away, still too stunned to speak, he asked, "What's wrong? Don't you think that'll work, keep 'em all closer to camp?"

"Yes. Yes, of course it'll work. And Madeline will save face with her friends. That's important at her age, to save face."

"For some people it's important at any age."

"Is it for you?"

He hesitated long enough to let Trudy know that already she had gone too far. It was like his telling her that he could give of himself, but she wasn't to pry or get greedy and grabby. He'd give what and when he could, but no more.

"Sometimes," he said finally.

Acting on inclination, she leaned toward him in the dark and pressed a kiss lightly to his lips. "Thank you," she murmured.

"For what? The girl?"

"For that and the advice and for being here and . . . for being who you are."

She stood quickly and left him, not knowing if he said anything in response, unsure whether she wanted to know if he did or not. She didn't want anything to spoil the moments they had shared. For her, Ian had given a whole new meaning to the camping concept of squatting in the bushes.

She sat by the fire for another half hour, listening

to the girls giggle and continue to tell bizarre stories until it became obvious that they might not ever go to sleep. She was a little too keyed up to sleep herself. Her mind was so full of Ian that she hardly noticed the ache in her muscles or the chill in the air as it whipped through her hair. However, she did notice the rain when the drops were big enough to splatter on her face.

A spitting rain rapidly progressed to a downpour. Lightning split the sky and thunder rumbled in Trudy's ears as she watched the leader in the Sunshine camp stick her head into the girls' tent to say something, zip it closed, and then scurry back to her own tent to squirrel in for the night.

Trudy's hair and coat were wet by the time she closed herself into her tiny shelter. She tossed the coat off, dried her hair as best she could with her towel, and scrambled into her sleeping bag to get warm, already sorry that she wouldn't have the additional insulation of her coat.

Knowing the way of her heart, she willed Ian's image to mind to generate more body heat.

"Ian!" She gasped suddenly, kicking her way out of her bag. She was back into her wet coat and sneakers before she realized what she was doing. She had long ago stopped feeling guilty for the uncontrollable things that happened to her, like rain on camping trips. But she was feeling pretty terrible that because of her Ian was now caught in the fallout of her misfortune.

The ground outside was slippery, and mud caked itself to her white tennis shoes.

"Ian?" she called in a loud whisper, trying not to arouse the other campers. She started on the stream side of the camp, where they had last been together, and followed the circling trees around to the other side. "Ian? Where are you?"

When her first sweep of the area didn't produce him, she cautiously moved farther into the woods, automatically accepting the very real possibility that she would get lost, contract pneumonia, and die in the total blackness before her.

But she couldn't stop looking for him, could she? She pictured him cold and alone, and called out again.

The lightning lit her way at irregular intervals, but her flashlight was of little use against the rain. On the far side of the cleared camping area she called out to Ian once more.

"Here," she heard him say, although it was hard to tell where he was.

"Where?"

"What are you doing out here?" he bellowed as a flash of light illuminated a small clearing where he hunkered under something big and bulky.

She maneuvered her way around the shrubs, bushes, and small saplings growing beneath the towering trees that surrounded the clearing, closing the distance between them before she spoke.

"I came looking for you. Come back to the camp with me. You'll die of pneumonia out here."

He didn't seem inclined to argue for a change, but hastily got to his feet, leaving everything behind but the sleeping bag he wore like a one-man tent. As if he were some huge bird, he swooped down on her with an arm and the bag extended wide to welcome her under his wing. "You're soaked. We'll probably both die," he said.

She glanced up at him as they raced toward the camp together and was about to reply to his prediction when she saw another flash of lightning strike high in the trees above them.

In the next two seconds everything seemed to happen at once. She saw the flash, heard the splitting of wood, knew a sudden terror, and pushed Ian away from her with all her strength. And then she felt nothing.

Six

The rain was all she heard. All she could see was darkness. Everything around her was real, still it seemed like a dream. She was in no pain, and yet she knew she was covered by a fallen tree. She didn't feel the heaviness one would expect with a tree upon one's chest, but she couldn't move either.

Walker was out of the mud and back on his feet before the loud thunk of falling wood left the air. Black shadows in the darkness melted together, forming indistinguishable shapes of various sizes, but none of them looked like a small woman standing alone and unharmed. Panic seized him, and he gave himself up to his instincts.

"Trudy?" His voice was a frantic echo in his ears.

"Ian? I'm under the tree," she called out, amazed to hear how calm her voice was. And then, suddenly, the tree was gone.

"Are you all right?" he asked. He wasn't sure how he came to have her dim, flickering flashlight, but he was shining it in her face as he turned it from side to side. Then he turned the light downward to inspect the rest of her. "Are you hurt? Do you feel any pain?"

"No. I don't feel anything."

"Oh, dear Lord." His heart twisted and fell like a stone in his chest. "You can't feel my hands?"

"Of course I can. But I don't hurt anywhere. I . . . I don't think it even touched me," she said in wonderment. She sat up and tried to look around. Her mind registered that it hadn't been a whole tree that had fallen on her, but a large, leafy branch that had come to rest on a fallen log behind her, trapping her in the space below. That's what her mind took in, but the rest of her didn't seem to be getting the picture. She still felt rather stunned and shaky.

Ian was dizzy with relief.

"Can you walk?" he asked. Slowly and in uneven stages, time fell back in a regular rhythm and events in an order Walker could comprehend. He was still feeling superenergized and mechanical in his responses, but thoughts were once again forming in his mind.

"Oh, sure," she said lightly as she felt the warmth of his hand close around the chill in her fingers. There was a gentle, solicitous quality in his voice that she'd never heard him use before. A semihysterical giggle escaped her. "I feel silly. I'm shaking like a leaf and I wasn't even hurt. Crazy, huh?"

"Shock." He automatically provided the diagnosis as the reality of what had just happened hit him. "You could've been killed."

Again she laughed lightly, incredulously. "Not this time."

Walker stood silently, staring at her through the darkness, unable to get a good look at her. Nausea gripped him. He swallowed hard and took a huge, gulping breath. He could recall the entire incident clearly, and although he didn't think she was aware of what she'd done, he was wholly cognizant of it.

Trudy had saved his life. Without motive or forethought she had jeopardized her own life to save his. She hadn't been paid to do it; it wasn't part of her job. It had been as spontaneous to her as her trembling was now. It was an unselfish act that came as naturally to her as breathing, and it shook Walker to the core.

He'd forgotten.

Trudy was like an antibiotic to a disease that had spread systematically through his heart and soul. For so long he'd been faced with the dregs of the world; he'd endured humanity in its most inhumane state and lived with the fact that in order to survive he had to become a part of it. Trudy was the antidote. From the first moment he'd laid eyes on her, she had poked at things long dead inside of him. He'd forgotten about the innate goodness most people possessed. He'd forgotten about truthfulness and innocence, idealism, kindness, and joy—all the wonderful things in life he'd set out to protect in the first place.

He'd watched her play with the girls and grow round-eyed listening to their ghost stories, and relived moments from his childhood that he hadn't thought of in years. Moments that warmed his heart and made him ache with nostalgia. She stirred emotions in him that were pure and uncalculated. The indebtedness he felt, the awe and gratitude he knew for the small, frail-looking woman before him clamped tightly around his throat and brought tears to his eyes.

"Ian? Are you all right?" she asked, worried by his long silence. "Did it hit you? Are you hurt?"

"I'm cold and wet. If you're sure you can walk, we'd better go," he said, lifting his face to the sky and inviting the rain to wash away the stinging sensation in his eyes.

Trudy let him turn her around in the direction of the camp and didn't pull away when his hand took hers. The fires were out, but flashlights and lanterns inside the tents told them they weren't entirely alone in the world.

Physically Trudy was unharmed. Emotionally it was as if she had met the grim reaper and laughed in his face. Her muscles were like rubber. Her heart couldn't beat fast enough, even though it was chugging like a steam engine. She felt superhuman and so full of life that she wanted to wake up the entire camp and have a party in the rain.

By the time Ian found Trudy's tent, she was feeling mighty high-spirited.

"It's a good thing we aren't allergic to mud, or we'd be dirty *and* itching when we got home tomorrow, and Helena would have a fit," she said, unaware that her rattling was reactive. "She might forgive the dirt if we tell her about the rain, but she'd be very suspicious of the itching. She'd think we had bugs, and she doesn't tolerate bugs at all, and as nice as she's always been to me, I don't mind telling you that I think she's a little intimidating sometimes. Just look at poor Charlotte. She's never said so, of course, but I think she'd like to work Ruby"—she laughed and shook her head—"I mean Roy. I think she'd like to work *Roy* into her act. But then Helena would be without a job, and she'd go stir crazy just sitting around the house. I've thought about it a couple of times, but I just can't come up with anything else for her to do."

"Hair spray," Ian injected absently, still rather preoccupied with his own reactions to Trudy's conduct back in the woods.

"What?"

"Hair spray," he repeated, trying to concentrate on the moment. "She could test hair spray in a wind tunnel."

Trudy gasped, and then she grinned. "Ian. That's very funny. Was that a joke? You were joking, right?"

"Yes," he said, a little perturbed that she couldn't tell the difference. "Shut up and get in before we drown."

He bent and held the flap of the tent open for her. She went in headfirst. "I don't think I've heard you make a joke before, Ian. Actually, I didn't think you had a sense of humor. I'm glad I was wrong, though.

I don't know how someone could live without a sense of . . . Ian?"

"What?"

"Aren't you coming in?"

"I'm getting undressed."

"What?" Her voice cracked in surprise.

"Just the wet stuff," he said. "Pile your shoes and coat in one corner and put on another pair of jeans. We've gotta get dry and warm, or we're going to get sick."

After mentally calculating exactly which parts of Ian's clothing would be wet, she shook her fists at the heavens in triumph and whispered an exuberant, "YES!"

She flipped off her muddy sneakers and coat and tossed them into the lower corner of the tent before scrambling out of her clinging wet jeans and into the sleeping bag, ignoring his advice about her spare pair of jeans.

She'd pulled a white sweatshirt on over her T-shirt when the night air had first started to get nippy. It was dry, but she shucked it off as well, and then rubbed her hands together in anticipation of Ian's grand entrance.

Her skin was tingling long before the wind whipped through the open flap to announce Ian's arrival. The flashlight had considerably more power in the confines of the tent, but what she saw made her face drop.

"You still have your pants on," she said. It sounded like an accusation.

"Well, I thought—"

"Oh, no you don't," she broke in, refusing to let her plans for Ian go awry. "You're not going to sleep in my sleeping bag with those wet jeans on."

"I wasn't going to—"

"Oh, sure," she broke in again, not allowing him to get more than four words at a time into the discussion. "I sleep in the bag and you sleep in those wet jeans, and then I go home healthy and you go home with a cold. You'd say it was all my fault and I'd never hear the end of it. I can tell you right now, Ian Walker, that's not going to happen. You take those jeans off and get into this bag or . . . or I'll put all my wet clothes back on again."

He was frowning at her darkly. She couldn't tell what he was thinking. She didn't really care. They were alone and it was unlikely that they would be disturbed. It was very hard to be guarded and stand-offish without one's clothes, and she wasn't about to let this perfect opportunity to get close to him go by.

Ian was clinging to the cold, wet material that encased his pelvis and legs as he would to a life preserver in a stormy sea. It was his plan to remain as uncomfortable as possible to keep his mind diverted from the comfort she could give him.

"That's stupid," he said.

"It's not any more stupid than your refusing to take your pants off." She gave him a considering look and smiled at him. "I promise I won't peek. And if it'll make you feel safer, you don't have to sleep in the bag with me. You can use the extra blanket Roy told me to bring."

Once again she crawled out of the sleeping bag, pretending that she had no notion of the effect her state of undress would have on Ian. She pulled the spare blanket out of the bag, tossed it to him, and then got back inside. She could hear his deep, irregular breathing from the other end of the tent.

He stared at her—hard, still seeing her in a tight T-shirt, bikini underpants, and socks.

"He said I'd be glad if I took an extra blanket, but I bet he didn't know how glad you'd be," she said, smiling at him.

"Who?"

"Roy, of course."

"Oh, yeah. Roy."

"Do you want me to turn the flashlight off too? Would that make you feel more comfortable?"

"I'm fine," he said, lying.

He'd taken his pants off for a hundred women, but none of them had watched as avidly as Trudy, and certainly none had caused him to feel such bashfulness. He accomplished the procedure in record time, wrapped himself in the blanket, and scooted up beside her.

"Happy now?" he asked. If he could have locked on to an emotion, it would have been anger. As it was, he felt scattered and disjointed. His body was screaming to touch her, to grab her up and love her until *she* screamed. But in his head and in his heart he wanted more for her. He wasn't sure of what. He just knew he wanted more.

"Yes. Very." Ecstatic was more like it, she thought as she squirmed down into her sleeping bag. She was trying to appear as if she didn't feel the tension between them, while her senses were leaping with excitement. She was trembling, but she wasn't cold and she was no longer in shock. She lay on her back and pulled the cover up to her chin.

"Good night, Ian."

"Good night," he said. He wanted to kiss her more than he'd ever wanted anything before, but he was afraid of what might happen if he did. The essential qualities of his manhood kept yelling take her, take her. But he kept hearing a faint, whispering voice in the back of his mind that murmured wait.

He tossed about for a comfortable position. When he found one, he reached across Trudy to turn off the flashlight.

Their faces came to within mere millimeters of touching. Black eyes met chestnut brown, and for endless moments Trudy felt as if they were trapped in an hourglass, she in one side, Ian in the other, with only the small opening between them. It was a tiny fistula that kept them apart but allowed little particles of who they were to flow freely back and forth and mingle with the other's. It was the few larger parts of their personalities, their secrets that kept them from joining as a whole.

The light went out, and she felt him settle beside her. The rain made little splattering noises as it fell on the tent.

"Ian?"

"I'm here, Trudy."

"I'm sorry."

"You are?" he asked, surprised by words he thought he'd never hear pass from her lips. And then he couldn't recall that she'd done anything to him recently aside from saving his life.

"I didn't mean for you to get rained on." She felt his arm slide across her abdomen. She swallowed in nervous excitement. He turned on the flashlight.

"Well, I'll be damned," he said, propped up on one elbow, staring down at her in disbelief. "After all the things you've done to me in the past three days you never once showed any remorse for, now you apologize for something that wasn't your fault."

"No, this time it was my fault. The other things were beyond my control."

"So. You're the one who controls the rain. I'd been told it was God."

"You still don't understand, do you?" she said, coming up on her elbow to face him.

"I guess not," he said, enjoying the perturbed look on her face. Compton had been right. Trudy had a face he never got tired of looking at. It was more animated than a cartoon, more dramatic than a sunset, and more entertaining than any movie he'd ever seen.

"Did you tell me you were coming out to the tent the night I Maced you, or did I ask you to come out and check on me?"

"No. But you should have known I might."

"I don't read minds, and nothing was said. What happened just happened, and it wasn't my fault. You could have just as easily been a hired killer. Shouldn't I have tried to protect myself?"

Instead of answering, he asked, "The wrench and the half a dozen times you've kicked me, poked me, or stood on my fingers? They weren't your fault either."

"That's right. I didn't throw that wrench at you, did I?" He shook his head and watched her sweet, soft lips as she spoke. "As for the rest, I believe in the sanctity of one's personal body space, and if you're in mine when I happen to be moving, then I'm not accountable for what might happen."

Ian wanted to slap himself. Her words were beginning to make sense to him.

"But this camping trip is different," she said. "I didn't *have* to go camping, and I knew that if I did, you'd insist on coming with me. And whenever I do something, I know there's always a chance that it might not turn out exactly as I have it planned. I hadn't planned on the rain, but I went camping knowing that you'd come with me and that something might go wrong. So your getting wet was my fault and I'm sorry."

He swallowed the laughter that bubbled in his throat and managed a sincere expression as he accepted her apology.

"You'd better tell me more about this personal body space of yours. That seems to be where I get myself into trouble most often," he said, amazed that he was actually enjoying such an absurd conversation.

"Well," she said, giving the subject some serious thought. "There's not much to tell, really. If you're in it, you're in it." Her face lit up with inspiration as Ian watched in delight. "Like the kiss you gave me last night. You didn't ask my permission or give me any warning that you intended to enter my personal space, so if I'd been chewing gum and you choked on it, it wouldn't have been my fault. But if I did that to you and bruised your face kissing you so hard, then it would be my fault. You see?"

"I'm afraid I do," he said. It didn't worry him that

he was beginning to understand her thought processes. But he *was* worried. "Did I hurt you last night?"

"No. I just wish . . ." She gave a slight shake of her head and broke eye contact. The kiss had been wonderful.

"You wish what, Trudy?"

She gave a soft, hesitant laugh, and when she spoke her voice was unsure. "You'll think this is crazy, too, but I'd never put kissing and anger together before. They sort of clash. They don't really go together, you know? And even though it wasn't a bad kiss, I . . . well, I wish you hadn't done it in anger."

Again she looked away. The truth was that she wished the kiss had meant more to him than simply a means of putting her in her place for the night.

Her breath caught in her throat when she felt his fingers under her chin. Gently he forced her to look at him. It didn't seem possible to her, but his eyes had turned darker than dark, like the fathomless black at the end of the universe. They looked as if they could suck her into a space devoid of air, time, and significance, yet they were gentle and tender.

"Is it too late to do it right?" he asked, his voice a deep, whispering caress.

Her lips parted, and Ian thought he might go mad in his longing before she gave him an answer. And then he saw it—the desire in her eyes that was just as hot and just as needy as his own, the tilt of her head that beckoned and promised, the faulty breathing, and the pulse point beating rapidly in her neck.

Like a parched and hungry man at a king's feast, he went slowly, hesitantly, toward his fare. He grazed her lips with his, savoring their softness and pliancy. He wet them with the tip of his tongue, relishing their sweetness. He sipped in and sucked on her fleshy lower lip and treasured the moment.

Trudy felt as if she were dying. Time stood still.

She couldn't hear or see. She wasn't breathing. Her entire body was beating to the rhythm of her heart, which seemed firmly lodged in her throat. She felt like an empty vessel waiting to be filled. And yet, if she were truly dying, then surely she was on her way to heaven, for she had never felt more rapturous.

The light touch of Ian's lips was like the brush of an angel's wing. His infinite gentleness illuminated her soul and rekindled the faith she had in her instincts. Her belief that a finer, more sensitive Ian existed under the harsh exterior was now a glorious reality.

Ian ended the kiss, but his hand continued to cup her cheek for the long moment it took her to open her eyes and look at him.

"Was that better?" he asked.

She nodded, lowering herself to the ground.

Ian put out the flashlight and lay down beside her, using vast stores of energy to control himself. The pain and pressure between his legs was unbearable. There was a gnawing ache in his chest. He clenched his teeth against the impelling forces that had built up within him and refused to give in to his cravings.

"Ian?"

"Hmm?"

"Is your whole life a secret? I mean, if I were to ask you about your family, could you tell me about them?"

"What do you want to know, Trudy?"

"I want to know about you. Where you came from. How you grew up. What you believe in. Who you are."

"Is that all?" His question was meant to be facetious, but in truth it was a stall. He wanted to tell her who he was. She'd saved his life and had a right to know. He simply didn't have many answers for her.

He used to. He used to think he had all the answers. He used to know exactly who he was and what he believed in and what he wanted out of life. But what used to be was a long time ago.

"If that's too much, just tell me what you can," she said, not wanting to put any pressure on their new and exciting but tenuous relationship.

"It's not too much, Trudy. I just don't know what to tell you."

"Start at the beginning and tell me everything."

He laughed in the darkness. "You'll be asleep in five minutes."

"I'm not the least bit sleepy. Tell me about your parents."

"They're dead."

"Ian."

Again he laughed, feeling more relaxed than he had in ages. Talking about his family was easy for him. They were good, kind people; uncomplicated, run-of-the-mill Americans who worked nine to five and raised their families.

As the rain began to subside he related parts of his early life to her in groggy, whispering tones. He told her about his childhood, his two sisters, and the highlights of his high school years. Soon he was recalling for her the cocky college graduate, newly enlisted in the navy, who flew off to officers' candidate school thinking he owned the world and came out a proud, idealistic, and somewhat naive young officer who wanted to defend the world with his life.

He covered the next few years briefly, mentioning how he'd come to meet her cousin, George Phillips, while working in naval intelligence. But the closer Ian came to the present, the sketchier his dialogue became. He was uncomfortable discussing this phase of his life with Trudy and skipped over huge chunks of time.

"Leaving the navy and becoming a federal operative was just the next step in a sequence of events. Since then I've been out of the country a lot, in a lot of different places, doing a lot of different things." He sighed heavily, having come to the end of his story.

Trudy was one of a handful of people who knew his history. He couldn't regret telling her as much as he had because it made him feel good to share the parts of his life he was proud of with her. As to the rest of his life, the greater part of the last twelve years . . . He wasn't too sure of how he felt about them anymore, only that he didn't want Trudy to know the specifics.

Trudy was warm and cozy in her sleeping bag inside the tent next to Ian. Outside, the night was quiet. His voice was all she heard. It had lulled her into a state of intimate companionship with him, and she felt comfortable and at ease with him for the first time.

She was also feeling a great deal of gratification. She'd been right about Ian all along. His tough, surly attitude was an act, something he wore like a coat of armor to keep people from finding out who and what he really was. The passion and vitality in his voice when he spoke of the people and the things he loved touched her and made her glow inside. Ian was no killer. She knew intuitively he was an understanding and compassionate man. Which then led her to wonder once again about his pain.

She tried to picture him in foreign countries being diplomatic or holding his pinkie in the air when he drank tea or bowing to kings and princes, but the image failed to develop. She couldn't see him doing any of those things, especially if he didn't hold with the nation's prevailing political or religious practices. He seemed to have a very low tolerance for tyranny and injustice and stupidity.

A sinking feeling in her chest told her that for Ian, being a government agent had nothing to do with statesmanship. Espionage seemed more in keeping with his outward appearance.

"I don't suppose you ever traveled to these countries on commercial airplanes," she said, fishing for more information to substantiate her suspicions.

"Sometimes. Why?"

He felt her body go rigid against his, and a fear greater than any he'd known before seized him. The silence between them grew thick with conjectures and dread before Ian realized that this was not the time to start running from his fears. If what he'd done appalled her, it was just as well to know about it now.

"Why'd you ask that, Trudy?"

She remained silent long enough for him to conclude that she had come to a few conclusions on her own and that her feelings toward him had changed drastically. He drew in a deep breath and braced himself for the moment.

"No wonder you don't like being called a mercenary. It's a little too close to the truth, isn't it?" she said, her voice aquiver with an emotion she was hard put to identify. Sadness was as close as she could come to naming the sick, useless feeling that shrouded her heart.

"No!" He couldn't see her, didn't want to see her, but he was sitting up and staring down at her nonetheless. A raging anger soared through him. He wasn't what she was accusing him of being, but she'd come too close to the truth. In many ways he wasn't much more than a soldier for hire.

He'd seen and done things he wouldn't tell a priest about, always telling himself that the ultimate goal was a good one, that his deeds could be justified in the name of duty, honor, and survival. But he had never enjoyed any of it, and he'd never been very proud of it. He had hoped that Trudy would never need to know.

"I'm not a mercenary. I didn't lie to you. A mercenary will kill for anyone who can pay his price. They have no loyalty. They don't believe in anything but money." How could he make her understand? Why should he bother? he wondered somewhere in the back of his mind. In the large scheme of things she was as insignificant as a grain of sand on a beach. And yet it was imperative to him that she comprehend *who* he was and not hate *what* he was.

"I believe in the United States of America, Trudy. I don't always agree with what she does, which is why I'm here with you, but I do believe in everything for which she stands. Freedom, democracy, civil rights, the right to choose and practice a religion—all that stuff they teach you about in grade school. I've been all over the world, and as screwed up as our government may seem sometimes, it's the best in the world. I'm proud to be an American. The damn flag sends chills up my spine, and one time I cried like a baby through the entire national anthem in front of a platoon of marines." He took a deep breath. The moment of truth had arrived. "I'd do anything for this country, Trudy. And the truth is, I've done it all."

Trudy couldn't stand it any longer. She was off the ground and had him in her arms before he could draw another breath.

"Oh, Ian. I am so sorry. I never dreamed it was something like this. I thought it was a woman, and then I thought it was just because you hated being with me. I had no idea. I'm so, so sorry. It must have been awful for you," she said, sobbing.

She held his head to her breast and wept into his hair. How many times had he been hurt? How many times had he betrayed his gentle, kind, and caring nature to defend what he believed in? Trudy's heart bled for him. How he must have suffered over actions that were abhorrent to him but that he'd sworn to perform in the defense of his country? Poor Ian. How could she ever soothe such pain?

Walker was floored by her reaction, and for several minutes simply allowed himself to be held and comforted. Gradually it came to him that she wasn't in the slightest way put off by his confession.

Did she truly understand? he wondered. This

flake? This airhead? This ditz? Was it possible that this one woman, this one-of-a-kind woman knew him better than anyone else in the world? Better than he'd known himself until just recently? Was she aware that every time he'd had to kill another human being, he'd kill a part of himself as well? How was it that in so short a time she knew what it had taken him years to realize?

"Trudy?"

"Yes." She sniffed loudly.

"I'm about to enter your personal body space again," he said as he took her face between his hands and drew it closer to meet his.

His lips pressed against her forehead and then each cheek, before his mouth closed over hers. He kissed Trudy with a tender, reverent thoroughness that obliterated every kiss she'd known before.

His hands slipped to her back and around her waist. She was like a spy in enemy territory, someone who knew too much, a threat. He held her close while he sapped the energy and strength from her small body to immobilize her. He took the air from her lungs and tortured her senses, searching for whatever it was that she possessed that allowed her such great insight and knowledge of his basic nature. She was completely dependent on him, and all he could do, all he *wanted* to do was cherish her.

He cradled her in his embrace as he lowered her to the ground. Adoring hands possessed her. They stroked her bare thighs and wandered across her abdomen, fantailing waves of exquisite pleasure in their wake. With his mouth he teased and tickled and tormented her, arousing her to a mindless, wild frenzy of need. His teeth nibbled at her engorged breasts through the T-shirt, and she whimpered for more.

She hardly noticed the size, shape, or tone of his body, but she was supremely aware that it was as warm and strong as his spirit. She longed to be closer to both of them, merge with them, and be safe and sheltered forever.

He felt a cold chill as her hands fell away from him. The soft, smooth skin of her abdomen touched his as she started to remove the rest of her clothing. His body clamored for completion. Still, he stayed her hands while he gave her one last, promissory kiss.

"Ian," she pleaded.

"We'll do it, baby. I want to make you feel so good. Shhh . . . I want to make you crazy for me. Drive you wild. But not now. Not yet."

"Please."

"Shh." He kissed her lightly, over and over. "There's more. You need to know all of it, Trudy. Then if you still want me, we'll make love until we're numb. We'll rest awhile, and then we'll do it all over again. Again and again."

"I don't want to know it all. I want—"

"I know what you want. And I'm going to give it to you. I'm going to give you everything. But I want it to be special this time. I want to make love to you as myself, not just who you think I am. I don't want there to be any secrets between us."

She released a resigned sigh at the urgency in his voice. "Couldn't we talk later?"

"No," he said, pulling away from her and drawing her T-shirt down to her underpants. He was a little bowled over by his own emotions, amazed at what he was doing. But it was important, and his decision felt right to him. Trudy was someone special, and he wanted to love her in a special way.

"All right, then," she said, cuddling close and laying her head in the crook of his arm, their faces only inches apart. "Do you speak as many languages as George?"

He laughed. "You don't have to know everything right this minute."

"Oh, yes I do."

"Aren't you tired?"

"Hardly," she said, not bothering to conceal the physical, emotional, and mental frustration she was feeling.

Again he laughed. He wouldn't have been able to sleep either. "Okay. Now, what was your . . . oh, yeah. Actually, I probably know a few more dialects than George. He doesn't get out of the office as much as he used to and . . ."

They talked until dawn. They had grown intimately familiar with each other's voice in the darkness and later with the angles and shadows of the other's face. It became easier to decipher emotions and reactions when the sun finally came up.

Ian spoke freely and spontaneously but was careful to listen and watch for Trudy's responses.

Trudy, on the other hand, was trying very hard to hide her revulsion of the life he'd led. Some of the things he'd been assigned to do turned her stomach. The lengths he'd gone to in completing his tasks outraged her. She kept trying to put herself in his place, to feel what he must have felt, but it wasn't in her. Nothing in her own life compared to it; even her vivid imagination failed her. And so she listened quietly, keeping her mind and heart open with sympathy and understanding and the belief in his basic goodness.

"Look at me, Trudy. Take a really good look and tell me what country you think I'm from," he said as if it were a dare.

He had pulled a corner of the dark brown blanket up over his head, leaving only his face exposed. He was sitting up, and Trudy had to roll over on her back to see him clearly.

"I don't know," she said, having given it no thought before. "You look like an Arab." She considered his dark eyes, hair, and skin, and then added, "Or maybe a Latin."

"That's right," he said, appreciating her astute perceptions. "I've been an Arab and a Latin. I've been an Israeli, a Turk, an Iranian, a Syrian, a

Bolivian, and most recently I was a Colombian. I have the dubious honor of being able to pass myself off as being of almost any nationality in the Middle East or from around the Mediterranean or south of the U.S. border—although I never mastered Portuguese, so I try to avoid the countries where it's spoken."

"Do you ever work with the F.B.I. or the C.I.A.?"

"Occasionally. But more often than not I work alone."

"So it's like being an undercover policeman."

"Yeah. Sort of."

"You sneak into a foreign country and blend in with the people. You check out the situation and then do what needs to be done—alone." Brooding over the danger he'd allowed himself to become embroiled in was like scratching a poison ivy rash. The more she scratched, the more irritated she became.

"No. Not entirely alone. We have contacts that get information in and out of the country for us. Safe places to hide, sometimes. And there's always a trapdoor, an escape route. They don't always work, but they're there." He hesitated for a moment, cautioning himself over the amount of information he was giving her. "There's usually a safety net too. Another agent who can step in, cause a distraction, and bring you in . . . home."

"George?"

Ian shrugged carelessly, reluctant to reveal the extent of George's involvement in his professional life. "Once or twice."

"That's the favor you're repaying him, isn't it? He saved your life—once or twice—and you're paying him back by protecting me."

Ian grinned. Then he leaned over her and pressed his lips to hers in a slow, sensuous kiss. "That's probably what George is thinking at this very moment. But the truth is, he did me another favor."

Seven

With the sun up and shining on another bright spring day, they slipped away from the campgrounds and back down the trail before the other campers slogged out of their mud-encrusted tents to start breakfast.

Walker led the way to the strong hot coffee at the first 7–Eleven he could find on the highway, and then he followed Trudy back into town. He realized that he should have been exhausted, but he wasn't. Just the opposite. He couldn't remember the last time he'd felt so good.

Telling Trudy about his life was more than being honest with her, it was cathartic for his soul. Hearing his story told out loud put a whole new perspective on it. He knew there were wounds that would never heal, but he also knew that eventually some would. He knew that he'd done some things that were not quite kosher and maybe even a little reckless lately, but he also knew that Special Agent I. N. Walker had performed many deeds that he could be proud of. He knew how his yesterdays had come to pass. He had a vague idea of what he wanted from tomorrow. And he felt that his today was the best he'd ever known.

Trudy decided camping hadn't been nearly as bad

as she'd thought it would be . . . well, actually, i
had been worse than she thought it would be, bu
at least she'd had Ian all to herself. She'd never
spent an entire night simply talking with a man
Then again, she'd never met anyone like Ian.

Ian. What an incredibly complex and intricate
man he was, she pondered, looking back at him
through the rearview mirror. He was a zealous man
with boundless compassion for the world around
him, a man with principles and beliefs, a man o.
great courage.

He wasn't exactly the man she'd pictured herseli
spending the rest of her life with, but the idea was
beginning to appeal to her. A quiet, decent man
with an adequate income and few demands was al
she'd ever prayed for. She should have known she'd
fall in love with a man who couldn't maintain a low
profile if an anvil landed on his face.

And was she in love with Ian? No. At least not in
love as she'd known it before. What she felt for Ian
was something far deeper, more pure and terribly
frightening. She had always enjoyed love before. It
made her happy. It made her see colors, hear music.
and feel everything more intensely. What she felt for
Ian hurt. His pain hurt her. Her need to be with
him ached. Her instinct to protect him and care for
him was fierce, wrenched from that part of her that
was basically animal. Thoughts of a world without
him were sheer mental anguish.

No. She wasn't in love with Ian. Part of Ian was a
part of her, a part of her she'd been searching for all
her life. He was her mind's companion, her spirit's
pleasure, and her body's mate.

She pulled the car over in front of her house and
watched as he parked his car behind hers. What
would he think if he knew what a coward she was?

"Have you grown roots in all that mud?" he asked
through the open window of her car. He viewed the
mud-splattered interior of her car with a weary

expression. "I'm too tired to clean mine up today. What about you?"

"I'm too tired to get out and face Helena." She let her head fall back on the headrest and groaned. "I can hear her now . . ."

"Where in blue blazes have you two been?"

They both turned their heads quickly to see Helena advancing down the walk, looking very much like a Sherman tank in an olive-green shirtwaist dress. Chowder, a living image of the working end of a dustmop, followed at a sedate pace.

"I thought that at least one of you would have enough sense to come in out of the rain last night," she said, glaring at Ian. "I stalled her as long as I could, but a decision had to be made by someone, so I made it. And just look at you," she squawked. "You're both muddy messes. She'll take one look at you and move out."

"Who?" It was a simultaneous question.

"The new boarder."

"What new boarder?" they asked as one again.

Helena took a deep breath and began to talk as she would to two mud-caked idiots.

"Sophie Williams is her name. She called yesterday morning right after you left, in answer to the ad for the room you had in the paper."

Ian frowned darkly at Trudy. "What ad?"

"The ad for the room I had placed in the newspaper."

"What room?"

"Your room, of course." She looked back at Helena. "It's rented?" she asked.

"I figured you needed the money."

"I do. You did just the right thing, Helena. Thank you. What a relief," she said, getting out of the car, her vitality restored. "I was beginning to think I'd never rent that room."

The two women started up the walk together, leaving an open-mouthed Ian at the curb.

"Hold it right there," he roared at Trudy. "What

the hell is going on here? Have you lost your mind? You can't take a perfect stranger in off the streets, when there could be a killer out there looking for you—not to mention what I'm supposed to do for a bed." Then he turned on Helena. "I'm taking Trudy into town for the next two hours, and that Williams person had better be gone by the time we get back."

With his hand wrapped tightly around her upper arm, Trudy was hard put to stop herself from being propelled back into her car. She dug in her heels and jerked her arm free, then turned to look up at him with a scowl that was as determined as his own.

"Now, you hold it, buster. I can't afford to lose this boarder. I have bills to pay. It's taken me six months to fill my house, and I'm not going to wait another six months just to satisfy my grandparents' paranoia." She looked thoughtful for a moment. Her voice was low and sultry when she spoke again. "I'm really glad now that it rained on our camping trip. Aren't you?"

"Yes," he said carefully. "But what does that have to do with this?"

She smiled at him wickedly. "Well, you're going to have to sleep *somewhere* now, aren't you?"

"Oh, for the love of Pete," Helena exclaimed. "I knew this was going to happen. The two of you have been making goo-goo eyes at each other since day one. I should have taken bets that this solitary camping trip wouldn't stay solitary for long."

"Well, for your information, Ian was a perfect gentleman, Helena," Trudy said with a dramatically indignant sniff as she stepped around the woman on her way to the house.

"Is that so?" Helena cast a disparaging look at Ian. "You got an old war injury, or what?" When Ian answered with a disdainful stare, she shook her orange wig and said, "I expected better of you, boy."

Her disappointment was nothing compared to Ian's when he met Sophie Williams. The woman was nearly as old as the hills and quite harmless-looking. Thin and withered, she didn't appear to have enough tone in her muscles to lift her hands off her lap, much less wield a weapon with which to harm Trudy. She wore thick tinted glasses and carried a huge knitting bag. Nothing about her created enough suspicion to warrant her removal from the house, especially if Trudy needed the income.

"My, what a handsome young man," the old woman said, releasing Ian's hand from a frail, friendly shake. "You remind me a little of my third husband with your dark coloring."

What could he say? "Where are you from, Mrs. Williams?" Force of habit more than mistrust compelled him to ask.

"Dansbury." She faltered, and then sat up straighter. "I've run away from home."

Ian almost left the room. He didn't want to touch that line with a ten-foot pole.

"My goodness," Trudy said, sitting down beside the woman, a solicitous arm snaking around her drooped shoulders. "What happened?"

When they discovered that the woman had taken flight from a nursing home where her son seldom came to visit her and more than once the attendants were caught going through her knitting bag, they instantly took her into the fold and said knitting bag became sacrosanct.

Ian listened for as long as he could, and then he went upstairs to move his belongings and clean up. He gathered up what few things he'd brought with him, packed them into his bag, and set it outside the bedroom door. A shower and a call to George would help, he decided, feeling vastly put upon.

George was out of the office. So it happened that it was Helena who stepped in to save Ian's day, by superseding Trudy's offer to make him a late breakfast.

"You run up and wash a few layers of that mud off you, and then come down for something to eat yourself," Helena ordered Trudy, with a you-owe-me-look for Ian.

"I'm not very hungry, but a bath sounds like heaven," Trudy said, yawning.

Charlotte and Ruby appeared and talked Helena into making breakfast for the two of them as well. It was a landmark meal, as breakfasts and lunches were always do-it-yourself, and Helena wasn't one to put herself out unnecessarily. Sophie joined them for tea, and the five of them sat around the dining room table like one big lampoon of a family—minus Trudy and Roy, of course.

When Trudy failed to appear after the meal—and a second fruitless call to George—Ian went to investigate. He found her wrapped in a damp towel, curled up like a child, sound asleep on her bed. His knees went weak as a great wave of tenderness passed over him. He stood for long moments simply watching her sleep.

She was like an angel who had fallen from the skies. A sweet, naughty little angel as basically good and pure as all the rest, who tried so hard to do all the things good little angels did, but who always seemed to fall a little short of the mark. It pleased him that she wasn't polished and perfect, that she thought in circles and that "things just seemed to happen to her." There wasn't a dull or predictable bone in her body. Everything about her was real and full of life.

He stepped into the room and closed the door. With hands that were easy and familiar with bodies of the opposite sex, he peeled the towel away from her to revel in the sight of her petite form. The pale, flawless skin and the contrasting triangle of coarse dark hair near the juncture of her legs tempted him to touch, to arouse the sleeping woman, and to take possession of all he strongly desired. His muscles were taut. His skin felt flushed and overheated. He regretted his noble qualms of the night before. Virtue had lousy timing, he decided.

When she shivered and groaned in her sleep, Walker smiled at the delicate emotions she unknowingly twisted around his heart. He tucked her under the bedcovers and sat down in the chair beside it to think and to watch over her.

Then he saw it. He bent closer for a better look and grimaced at a scar that began on her shoulder blade and extended five inches down her back. It was an old wound, the skin was barely pink along the thin incision line. But his heart beat heavily at the evidence that she had once endured extreme pain.

Slowly he slid back into the chair, wondering about other pains she hadn't told him about, what else he didn't know about her.

She had almost decided not to wake him. He looked peaceful, if somewhat uncomfortable, slouched down in the overstuffed chair. His thick lashes were dark against his cheeks, curling upward on the ends; his usually keen and watchful expression was relaxed and calm in sleep.

She smiled a little and blushed self-consciously, remembering the state of her undress when she'd come awake. Longing twisted deep and low in her abdomen.

She'd always been grateful for the life she led. It was a full existence with people who loved her, new experiences to challenge her, and the perpetual notion that what few crosses she'd been forced to carry in her life, others had borne far heavier. She'd made her mistakes, she'd known loneliness, pain, and fear, but *always* she'd had hope as well.

She slid from the bed to the floor, positioning herself between his outstretched legs. Recalling the last time she'd surprised him, she was careful not to touch him. She leaned forward and placed a feather-light kiss to his lips. His eyes came open as if he'd been waiting for her touch. He didn't move, but he let his gaze roam over her body.

"You're dressed," he said. There was trace of disappointment in his voice that thrilled Trudy. He pushed himself up in the chair, extended his arms above his head, and pulled on the cramped muscles in his back and shoulders. He sat forward while lowering his arms, and they fell naturally around Trudy's waist to draw her closer. "I wish you hadn't done that."

"I wish I'd known you were going to wish that I hadn't done it. Then I might not have," she said, smiling into his eyes, feeling as if she'd known him forever. "Next time leave a note."

"Uh-uh. Next time I catch you like that, you're mine."

Her hands went to the buttons on the front of her cotton shirt and pretended to set to work. "That's easy enough to arrange."

Ian laughed. "Haven't you ever heard of playing hard to get?" he asked, teasing her, beaming at her enthusiasm.

"Sure. But if we both play at it, we'll never get anywhere."

"Is that what you think I've been doing? Playing hard to get?" With an inviting tug he coached her onto his lap, facing him. "Because if it is, you're dead wrong, sweetheart. I'm as easy to catch as a cold. All you have to do is say you want me."

He spoke the words lightly, but their implication and the look in his eyes were heavy-duty. He wasn't talking casual, uncomplicated sex. He wasn't a casual, uncomplicated man. And it was too late for Trudy to turn back. What she felt was more uncasual and complicated than anything she'd ever known before. It was complex and indefinable, it entangled her life so completely that it altered the basic core of who and what she was. It was frightening, but there was also an unerring certainty and infallibility to it.

And so it was with confidence and a sense of the absolute that she uttered the words "I want you."

Ian felt strangely humbled, but not enough to keep him from taking what he wanted. Where Trudy's fingers had pretended to unfasten the buttons down the front of her shirt, his did so in earnest. With great deliberation the first two were released to expose her delicate skin and the sloping ripeness of her breasts.

Like an awe-struck youth with his long-awaited first automobile, he regarded the fine craftsmanship of her breasts and then reached out to mindlessly stroke the contours, to feel their warmth and softness against his fingers. The privileges and the responsibilities of his new ownership were not lost to him in the glory of the moment. He sought Trudy out in the depths of her eyes and found her waiting for him, open, accepting, and vulnerable. Intuitively he knew that if he placed his heart at the mercy of hers, she would nurture and protect it, insure its safety from all harm.

Ian touched Trudy's cheek as if she were the most precious thing he'd ever encountered. He made her feel that way. He rose up to kiss her, and she felt all the loose pieces of her life settle gently into place. He ignited her heart and pumped liquid fire into every nook and cranny of her being. Like mortar in a brick wall, he filled her empty spaces and made her feel strong and whole.

She framed his face with her hands and sipped sensuously on his lips. His five o'clock shadow was much older after a day in the wilderness. It felt rough and earthy against her palms. Reality swayed out of focus. His short beard tickled her nose and chafed at her chin, but she hardly noticed.

The deeper he kissed her, the more pleasure she felt. The more pleasure she felt, the greater the pain of her need became. She wrapped her arms around him and pressed her body closer. He held her tight. With his lips he traced the line of her jaw.

She gave herself up to the moment. There was no killer stalking the yard below her window; there was no tomorrow, no past. Only the moment and Ian existed. She was vaguely aware of his hands on her belly. Electric knots coiled inside her. Her neck grew weak as he dotted it with soft, wet kisses, her head lolled to one side. She peeked out at the world, found it spinning, and quickly closed her eyes again. With his tongue he drew a trail down the valley between her breasts. Air caught in her throat. Her mouth was so dry.

With her fingers laced through his thick black hair and the scent of him forever in her memory, she lifted his face to hers once more. The kiss was long and hot. Relief and excitement surged within her as cool spring air drifted across her back and shoulders. Her blouse was gone. She opened her eyes when she felt the hook on the front of her bra give way. Ian was watching her.

If the intensity of his gaze frightened her the day they met, by all rights she should have fainted dead away at what she saw. Passion, be it called rage, desire, or love came in only one degree of intensity. Extreme. But what she viewed in Ian's gentle expression and fierce, dark eyes caused her no fear. She smiled at him.

She couldn't help it. It was a natural thing to do. Knowing the man to whom you belonged, after years of wondering if he even existed, called for a smile. Actually her whole body was smiling. She felt as if she were splitting at the seams with emotions she could never get enough of. Exhilaration and contentment. Yearning and eagerness. And . . .

"I love you," she said, her voice thick and throbbing with the effort it took for her to speak.

For an instant the fire in his eyes raged out of control, it faded and softened, and then came back brighter than ever. Something wild and consuming broke loose in him. In one rapid, fluid motion he was out of the chair with Trudy in his arms, his mouth pressed hard against hers, his tongue stroking hers as he pulled at her life's breath, and then he lowered them together onto the bed.

He kissed the thoughts from her mind. He frazzled her senses as he cupped her breast and tormented the hard, aching tip with his fingers. She gasped for air. Her body arched in ecstasy. He wrapped both arms around her and lowered his head to her breast. His beard scratched her. He nibbled and sucked. She was hot and damp. A biting hunger, pulsating deep and low in her pelvis, brought her hips off the bed. She felt the warmth of his skin against hers and didn't give a second thought, much less a first thought, as to how he'd disposed of his shirt.

Her hands pressed and pulled along his back and across his broad shoulders. She wanted to merge her body into his, become one with him because her instincts told her that only he could put an end to the infinite emptiness she was feeling.

"Trudy? Are you in there?" Charlotte's voice came loud and clear from the other side of the door. She rapped hard, as if it weren't the first time she'd tried to get Trudy's attention.

"Aw, for crying out loud," Walker muttered as he rolled his body away from Trudy's, aware that the spell had been temporarily broken.

"Ah. Yes?" Trudy called.

"Have you seen Mr. Walker? There's a phone call for him," Charlotte said.

"Oh, for pity's sake, Charlotte. Who are you trying to kid? The two of them have been locked in that room all day long. Of course she's seen him," they heard Helena say. And then in a louder voice she said, "Put your pants on, boy. You got a phone call, and he won't leave a message."

"Mother! I was trying to be polite," Charlotte said, her voice softer as she moved away from the door.

"Why? They . . ." Thankfully Helena moved out of hearing range.

"Damn," he said with a slow shake of his head as he lay on his back, looking up at the ceiling. His breathing was still ragged; his body trembling with unspent energy. "There's nothing like a little privacy, huh?"

"I'm sorry." She rolled close to him and laid her arm across his chest, trying to hug him.

He enfolded her in his embrace and held her near his heart. "No. I'm sorry." Then he laughed. "Do you suppose anyone in this house would believe that we haven't had sex yet? That so far all we're guilty of is making love?"

"I don't think so."

"Me either," he said, releasing her gently and coming to a sitting position. He looked back at her half-dressed body with a wry smile. "I hate being accused of something I didn't do, so don't go away. I'm coming right back to commit the crime."

"Hurry."

"Hey, pal. What's up?" It was George returning Walker's call.

"Hardly anything anymore," he said with regret as he adjusted the fit of his jeans. "What have you heard about Packston?"

"Not much. I guess he's waiting to see what'll happen at the appeals hearing. Everything is very quiet on that front." He paused briefly. "Why? What's happened?"

"Nothing. But I want you to check out somebody for me, and if you laugh, I'll inflict a great deal of pain on your face."

"This ought to be good."

"Why do you say that?"

"Well, the last time you asked me to do this, I dug up something very interesting."

"What?" Automatically the nerves in Ian's neck grew tense and ready to react.

"Nothing serious. But you might want to take a

closer look at this Roy person and his sister. He's been arrested a couple of times on misdemeanor charges. And I couldn't find *anything* on her."

Walker frowned. For a second he thought he heard humor in George's voice, but then it was gone. "What kind of misdemeanors?"

"Relax. It's nothing serious. Just keep your eyes open."

Click. Click.

Ian knew the noise that had come faintly over the line. He cast his gaze quickly over the vicinity and strained his ears to hear it again. George, too, had heard the sound and had fallen silent on the other end.

"I'll take care of that," Ian said. It was his way of telling George that he would eliminate any devices being used to monitor their conversation. "Check out a Sophie Williams. Last known address is a nursing home in Dansbury."

"A nursing home? You want me to check out someone from a *nursing home*? Like how many operations she's had? Whether or not she's taking laxatives? What do you want here?"

Ian sighed. Checking out Sophie was probably crazy, but he was used to doing a thorough job. Besides, there was always a one in a zillion chance that she was an ex-mob moll or something.

"Just do it, George."

"O-*kay*. Anything else? Is Trudy still trying to kill you?"

"No." Actually it was killing him just thinking of her, but George didn't need to know that. "I'm safe as long as I stay out of her personal space."

"Good. Can't imagine what you'd be doing in it in the first place."

Ian hung up the phone, waited a second or two, and then took the receiver apart looking for a bug. He found nothing, which meant it was an outside wiretap. He felt a modicum of comfort in knowing that whoever was tapping the phones was still in the monitoring stage. Then again, the continued surveillance made him wonder why they were waiting. If they knew where Trudy was, why didn't they come after her?

If someone was going to try to kill Trudy, he wanted them to make their move as soon as possible. He wanted it over with. He hated waiting. But more than that, he wanted the freedom and peace that would come when Trudy was no longer in danger.

He followed Helena's and Charlotte's voices into the kitchen. The rest of the house seemed deserted.

"Anyone have a problem with me spending the night on the couch tonight?" he asked. He strode into the room as if he hadn't recently been interrupted in the throes of passion with his subject, as if he hadn't just encountered the first evidence that Trudy's life was indeed in peril, as if it were an ordinary Sunday evening in late spring.

"Would it make any difference if we did?" asked Helena.

"Nope." He gave Sophie a polite nod of recognition when he saw her sitting at the kitchen table, rubbing her knitting needles together in a slow, arthritic fashion.

He perused the contents of the refrigerator, hoping to find something of interest to take back to Trudy as a peace offering. He had a feeling she wasn't going to like the idea of his sleeping on the couch any better than he did. Nothing appealed to him.

"Anybody know where Roy and Ruby are?" he asked casually. They were the only boarders still unaccounted for.

"Anybody care?" Helena asked as she sat down at the table with a submarine sandwich that looked made to scale. She placed a smaller version in front of Sophie. "Eat up," she instructed her.

"Mother!" Charlotte said, a scolding frown on her pretty face. She turned to look at Walker. "They're rehearsing tonight. They'll be home at the usual time."

"What's Ruby rehearsing? What does she do, anyway? Is she part of his act?" Strange. Why hadn't he questioned her livelihood before this?

"Yes . . . sometimes. She's part of his act sometimes, yes," she said, stammering. For all her normal appearance, Charlotte struck Walker as being just as weird as the rest of the residents.

"I see. Well, I hope they come in quietly. I'd hate to shoot them by mistake," he said in jest. And when it became obvious that no one, including Helena, thought it was funny, he muttered, "It's an old F.B.I. joke. Sorry."

A few minutes later Walker let himself into Trudy's room. Closing the door became reflex when he stopped dead in his tracks at the sight of her. His arousal was strong and immediate. She had removed the rest of her clothes and covered herself with the pale pink bedsheet. She was sitting up, waiting for him.

"Uh," he groaned, miserable. *Why me?*

"What's wrong?" she asked, her welcome smile fading.

He let loose a loud sigh and walked across the room to be close to her. "Something's come up. I, we . . . we'll have to take a raincheck on this."

"I thought this was the raincheck," she said, her disappointment as plain as his. "I thought . . ."

"I know what you thought, sweetheart. And believe me, that same thought hasn't been far from my mind since the first time I laid eyes on you. But this can't be helped. Now isn't the right time."

"Well, for pete's sake, Ian. How will I know when it *is* the right time? Should I consult a psychic or an astrologer? Watch for full moons?" she asked, frustrated once again.

He laughed. He couldn't stop himself. The only

other alternative he had was to cry. He grabbed her up into his arms and held her near to him.

"Please try to understand. I can't explain it just now, but I will. And as soon as everything is settled, we'll be together. I promise, Trudy. I promise."

She allowed him to hold her while her semitattered mind tried to sift through the facts. Was he toying with her? No. She knew an eager man when she saw one. Had she done something to offend him? No. He was holding her in that gentle, adoring way that she was fast becoming addicted to. What had happened while he was gone?

"George," she muttered against his chest. She pulled away to look up at Ian. "Has his timing always been this bad?"

Amused by her thinking, he said, "He usually shaves it pretty close, but he's never jumped the gun on me before. He's getting pretty old, though. I tell you what. How about if I take you out to dinner tonight. I think you ought to make me wine you and dine you before you let me have my way with you. Don't you know how any of this works? First you play hard to get, then you make me wine and dine you, then you hem and haw for a while. What's the matter?"

"What did George say?" The serious expression on her face and the dread in her eyes made him feel sick. He was going to enjoy snapping the neck of whoever was doing this to her. This time he wouldn't think twice about it.

"Not much, baby. Don't worry. Get dressed and come out with me. I'll tell you all about it."

Eight

"So. It's really going to happen, then," Trudy said. She had been hoping against hope that the situation would prove to be benign. She felt a little stunned and sick knowing that the worst fear she now had was about to become a reality.

"I'll have George check the source of the wiretap. That'll tell us something. Outside taps aren't as easy to accomplish as placing a bug in the phone. It'll give us a better idea of who we're dealing with," Walker said, trying to sound calm as his mind conjured up everything that could go wrong. There were several scenarios to choose from, but they all culminated in the same end. Trudy's death.

He couldn't let that happen. He wouldn't let it happen. Keeping Trudy safe was the mission of his lifetime. He'd die before he failed.

"I'll check the rest of the house for listening devices tonight," he said, watching her push her untouched food back and forth across the plate with her fork. "You know, it's not too late, Trudy. We can put you in protective custody, and then after the trial you can go away and start a whole new life, leave all this behind you."

"No."

"Why not? Trudy, this is crazy. You might be lonely for a while, but at least you won't be dead."

"Yes, I would be. I'd be dead inside. I'd know what a coward I was and I'd hate myself. That's worse than being dead."

"Not in my book. Besides, taking precautions isn't cowardice, it's smart. You only get one ride on the merry-go-round, sweetheart. You want to make it last as long as possible."

She fell silent. She couldn't argue with what he was saying, but she couldn't run away and hide either.

For a few short, blissful moments she had envisioned herself starting a new life with Ian. In his arms it had been easy to forget who she was. When he kissed her, danger didn't exist.

"I can't live like that," she said. "But I would certainly understand if you wanted to pull out. I don't think you or George knew what you were getting in to when you agreed to help me. And considering the way things have been going in my life lately, there's a very good chance we could both wind up dead."

"Stop that," he said, instantly angry. "I don't mind playing this out your way, but I won't listen to self-pity. And compared to some of the tight squeezes I've been in, this'll be like a lark for me. You stick close to me, and we'll make out just fine. You'll see."

He felt like a big talker, considering that he was putting the most important person in his life on the line. But he didn't want her to give up hope. He still had some, and he'd hang on to it until he drew his last breath.

"I'd die anyway if anything ever happened to you," she said, trying to convince him to be cautious.

"Nothing's going to happen to either of us," he said, hoping he sounded sure of the fact. He laughed softly and tried a new approach. "We haven't even made love yet. I refuse to die until after we've made love a few thousand times."

She picked up on and appreciated his effort to lighten the mood. "Men! Is that all you ever think about?"

"It's all I ever think about when I'm looking at you. How am I going to get her into bed? How many ways can I drive her crazy with passion?"

"You wanna go home now?" she asked, eager to count the ways.

He laughed. "Nope. We need to stop in and see ol' Horace Turner first and let him know what's going on. He'll need to keep his eyes open as well. Which reminds me, we'll need to get Helena and Sophie and the others out of the house until this is over. Witnesses are usually as expendable as the victims."

"I tried before, but maybe now that we know there really is someone out there . . ."

"I'll have a talk with them," he said as he watched her anxiety increase. "If you're not going to eat any of that, we might as well leave."

They made the short journey across the town of Victory to the sheriff's office in oppressed silence. Walker wanted to say something clever to amuse and entertain Trudy, but nothing came to mind except an offhand reference to her uncharacteristic silence. As much as her incessant chatter had irritated him when they'd first met, he'd grown accustomed to it, had been charmed by it. He felt useless and dejected seeing her so quiet and bottled up.

Every bone in his body was telling him to pack her up and secret her away somewhere until he could make the world safe for her again. He couldn't understand why she was putting herself through the torment, when all she had to do was consent to a witness protection program.

He'd changed his identity a hundred times, and it was only recently that he'd lost sight of who he truly was. Her circumstances wouldn't be as difficult. Trudy would always be Trudy, but for one new name and one new life. How attached could she be to a name and a house full of kooks? he wondered.

He drove the car into the parking lot beside the sheriff's office, relieved to see that Horace Turner's car was parked out front. He'd feel a little better knowing he had the old ex-marine watching the house from the outside. But there was something nagging at him in the back of his mind. Before Trudy could get out of the car, he stopped her.

"Wait a second," he said.

In answer, she turned to look at him. The flood-lights showed him the dull, lifeless expression in her eyes.

"When I talked to your grandparents the other day, they told me that you wouldn't go into the protection program because you'd run away from something before and lost everything. What was all that about?"

"Nothing, really. I can't believe they told you that," she said, her voice low, her gaze diverted from his.

"Was it a lie?"

"No. Not exactly. I did tell them that, but . . ."

"What?"

"It was a long time ago. It doesn't apply anymore. Things have changed. Everything is different."

"Tell me about it anyway."

She released a deep, resigned sigh, and looked straight ahead. Her weakness warned her to lie, to run and hide the true state of her nature from him. But how could she not tell him the truth? He had bared his soul to her, entrusted her with his shame. How could she lie? She loved him. In the face of all the courage he'd expended for the truth and decency he believed in so completely, it was time he knew what a cowardly person she was.

She leaned back against the headrest and began to speak in a low, even tone of voice.

"People have told me that my parents were very dedicated to their faith, that they were a very religious couple. But if someone were to ask me if that was the truth, I'd have to admit that I don't know. They weren't around enough for me to find out."

"They died when you were young?" he asked, empathetic to her loss. He couldn't help wondering what her parents had to do with her reasons for not accepting government protection, but he was getting used to her circular thinking and held on to his belief that she would eventually get to the point.

"I was nine. And I do remember some things about them, but not what kind of people they were. Just feelings and impressions, you know?" She paused as if to recall them to mind. "I remember wanting to please them. I wanted them to like me and to be proud of me so we could live together and be a regular family."

"Sweetheart, I don't understand. Where were they? Why didn't you live with them?"

She looked at him as if to imply that she'd already covered that part of her story and he hadn't been listening—and then she realized she hadn't.

"They were missionaries."

"Missionaries?"

"I was born in South Africa," she said. "When I was two, my parents brought me back to the United States because of the racial unrest there. I guess they wanted me to be safe. Well, I'm sure *now* that's what they had in mind. But for the next seven years I lived with my grandparents and my parents would come home for a few months and then leave again. I added it up once. Including the first two years, I was with them for three years and four months before they died when I was nine."

A wistful expression crossed her face, and Ian frowned, once again realizing how little he knew of the pain in her life. She was always happy and bubbly, always cheerful and optimistic. He had simply assumed that there had been very little strife in her existence. The scar on her back and the story of a lonely childhood led him to believe that there was even more to the Trudy he had come to know and consider as someone very special.

"I remember how excited I used to get when

Granny would tell me they were coming home," she
went on to say. "I'd think, 'maybe this time they'll
stay, and we could be a real family, like all my
friends have.' I'd work extra hard on my studies so
they'd know how smart I was. I made sure that I
didn't get into any real trouble so they wouldn't hear
about it when they got home. And my room." She
laughed. "My room was spic and span for weeks
before they arrived. I tried so hard to be the perfect
little girl so they'd want to stay and be my real parents instead of a couple of strangers who sent letters
and these weird presents from places I'd never even
heard of."

She turned her face away from Walker to stare
out the car window. He automatically reached out to
comfort her. He slid his hand behind her neck and
gently turned her head toward him.

Looking into the unique face that had come to
mean more to him than his own life, he stroked her
cheek tenderly and murmured, "What happened?"

Trudy rubbed the side of her face against the palm
of his hand, wondering if he'd ever be able to understand what she so desperately wanted to tell him. It
had taken her twenty years to forgive herself for
what she had done. Could he at least understand
it?

"The summer I turned nine, they came home for
three months," she started. She cleared the emotional lump from her throat and strove to speak in
a clear, dispassionate tone of voice. "It was wonderful for a while. I remember sitting out under that big
tree in my grandparents' front yard with my mother,
having long talks and thinking that maybe she did
love me after all. My father was a minister, and he
preached at the church almost every Sunday. I
couldn't recall him ever doing that on his other vis-
its, so I began to believe that they were going to stay
with me.

"Then one day they announced that they were taking me to Zimbabwe with them. I think they must

have discussed it with my grandparents before-hand, because they didn't seem as surprised as I was. But as a nine-year-old, I perceived their lack of surprise as indifference. I tried talking to both of my grandparents, but all they kept saying was that my parents knew what was best and that I'd become accustomed to their way of life.

"It was so long ago that I don't really have memories of it anymore, just feelings. I felt very, very alone. I didn't really know my parents. I don't think I trusted them. They kept leaving me. What if they left me in Zimbabwe? I didn't even know where the heck Zimbabwe was. But I knew what I had, and even though my grandparents were acting as if they didn't care about me, I knew I could trust them. I had my school and my friends. Everybody in town knew who I was, and I felt safe there. I just couldn't face going to some strange place, to a strange school, to speak a strange language with a couple of people who were all but strangers to me," she said, emphatic and emotionally stressed. Then suddenly all her energy seemed to drain away. "So, I ran away," she whispered.

An affectionate smile found its way to Walker's lips. For a terrified nine-year-old to run away from home didn't sound like such a great sin. There wasn't anything to read between the lines either. Everything she'd felt at the time seemed pretty natural to him.

"Where'd you go?" he asked.

"I remember getting the shots for the passport too," she said absently.

"What happened then, Trudy?"

She took a deep bracing breath. "I'm not sure. My granny and my mother were in my room packing all my things into boxes and suitcases, and I went out to sit in Grandpa's work shed. I sat there for hours and hours, watching a little brown spider crawl back and forth across the wall. I heard them calling for me when it started getting dark, but I didn't answer them. I kept wishing they'd leave without me.

"It was dark outside when my grandfather found me. I wouldn't leave the shed. I think I might have gotten a little hysterical, because I remember feeling very cold and I was crying and screamed something at my mother, but I don't remember what. And then all at once they were leaving . . . without me."

"You felt abandoned again."

"Lord, no. I was glad they were gone. I hoped they would never come back and try to take me away again. I remember the relief." She was silent for several minutes. Suddenly she said, "Their plane crashed on the way to Zimbabwe."

"That wasn't your fault," he said, quick to put the puzzle pieces together in his mind. She couldn't possibly still believe that her wish had caused her parents' death, could she? he wondered. Twenty years was plenty of time for her to realize that wasn't the case.

"I know," she said, although she could recall anguishing over the fact that it had been. "That was when my grandmother told me about my knack for being in the wrong place at the right time."

"But you were in the right place at the right time."

"Not technically. I should have been with my parents. They had wanted me with them so that we could be a real family, the way I wanted. I was in the wrong place at the right time, and it saved my life."

But was it a life worth saving? For a long, long time she hadn't thought so. The shame and remorse she had bottled up inside her for rejecting her parents and allowing their last memory of their daughter to be that of a coward ate away at her. She had spent the next fifteen years in a blur, trying to prove to herself that she wasn't totally without courage.

That phase of her life had ended in disaster as well, but she had come away with the knowledge that fear was sometimes a good thing and that when pressed to a point beyond her control, she could and would do anything to survive. Life had always been precious to her, and trying to protect her own existence was no disgrace, even though it had seemed rather cowardly then.

It was some time before she could look at Ian. She was concerned about what he was thinking. He was so idealistic and so brave and so willing to take horrible risks with the life he had that she felt sure he would never understand that she couldn't do the same thing.

He was watching her closely, and when their eyes met, she found no scorn. He looked serious and thoughtful but not condemning.

"Well, I'm glad you were in the wrong place at the right time, but the witness protection program isn't the same as running away and hiding, you know," he said gently, thinking he knew the reason for her refusal to accept the government's help.

"It isn't?" The question was ambiguous.

"All right, maybe a little. Protecting yourself is protecting yourself, and there's nothing wrong with that."

"But it's also giving up everything and everyone you love. It's also living in constant fear of being discovered. It's also pretending to be someone you're not and never being able to be honest with people. And it's also very lonely. What kind of life is that?"

"It's a life," he said. "It's better than being dead."

"Just barely," she said. "And besides, I'm not going to die."

His dark brows rose in interest. "What makes you so sure of that?"

"Well," she said, dragging out the word for added suspense. "Seeing as how it's your job to make sure nothing happens to me, I've come to the conclusion that you probably won't let me compromise your state of alertness by letting me seduce you. *And* seeing that you've promised to make love with me at least once before one or the other of us dies, it stands to reason that you'll think of some way to get us out of this fix. You *are* a man of your word, are you not?"

She was grinning at him, daring him to argue with her. Instead, he leaned across the seat and bussed her lips.

"You're an impossible woman, Trudy Babbitt."

"That's a matter of opinion, Ian Walker. *Not* the answer to my question. Are you a man of your word or not?"

"I try to be," he said, and then he kissed her again, sweetly and gently, as he tried to show her how much she'd come to mean to him—then deeply as he relayed his singular desire to obsess her mind, possess her body, and cherish her most unusual heart.

They found Horace Turner in his office with his feet propped up on his desk, hiding from the world behind a newspaper. He seemed relieved to see them.

"Where you two been? I just got back from taking a swing by your house. One of the cars was missing, so I stopped in to see how things were goin'. That redheaded witch answered the door. Told me you'd gone out to eat. Got some news for ya."

He had their undivided attention but waited for them to ask what his news was anyway.

"You told me to check out any new faces that came through town," he said, looking at Ian. "Well, I been watchin', and there's been two. The old lady that moved into your house and the cab driver who brought her here."

"And?" Ian coached when it appeared Horace had gone as far as he could on the first question and needed another.

"They're both from Dansbury. The cab driver got gas and went straight back. He lives at 1265 Bea-con—"

"What else?"

"Well, I felt real dumb checking up on that old lady, but you said *everybody.*"

"Right."

"She's registered at the Creek of Peace Nursing Home, but I'm guessin' that they hadn't discovered she was missin' by the time I called, cuz they told me she wasn't takin' any phone calls."

Ian thanked him for his efforts and went on to tell him about the wiretap on the phone. The rest of their conversation was lost on Trudy as her mind began to wander.

How long would it be before the assassin made his move? How would he do it? Would he be quick or would he deliver a message from his employer first? A hundred such queries filled her brain until she heard Ian say something that brought her back to the present.

"This isn't a half bad job you have here, Turner. I've been thinking of hanging up my cloak and dagger and getting one like it for myself."

Trudy couldn't tell if he was serious or not, but Horace apparently thought he was.

"Hell, boy, you can start here tomorrow. I'll train you as my deputy, and in two years time you can have this desk, cuz I'll be retired."

"Really?" Was that actually interest in his voice? Trudy wondered. She sat and watched him with a confused frown on her face, refusing to give hope to the notion of Ian's staying on once his debt to George was paid. "I'll think about it," he said.

Horace walked them out to the car. He stretched his large body and smoothed his shirt down over his belly. "Well now, you two keep an eye out, and I'll have one of the girls down at the telephone office check locally for that bug. Let you know as soon as I hear anything. And I think I'll make a couple extra passes through the neighborhood for the next few days. Still think you ought to call in the troops on this one, though."

"No. More people around would only scare him off or get people killed. What I would like to do is empty the house. I'd especially like to get rid of that Methuselah who got my bed," Walker said in jest, no longer begrudging the old lady the room. The only bed in the house he wanted to sleep in was Trudy's. Unfortunately until this mess was settled, he'd need his wits about him—which left him on the couch.

"I'm going to *disregard* that statement about my newest guest," Trudy said in a loud, commanding voice. "Besides, Methuselah was a man, not a woman."

"Sorry," he said, a brow raised at her sudden sensitivity about her boarder. He exchanged a bewildered look with Horace Turner, who puckered his lips and shrugged.

Without realizing what he was doing, he reached around her to open the car door. She was of the same mind, but backed off when she saw his hand. Walker saw stars when her head bashed into his jaw.

Nine

Trudy and Walker returned to the boardinghouse, nervous and wary. It was after nine o'clock and everyone seemed to be settled in their rooms for the night. The silence was eerie. Together they crept to the second floor to do a bed check.

Sophie's room was dark, and from the sounds of her deep, rhythmic breathing, she appeared to be asleep. Helena, looking like a character from Creature Feature Theater in her bedclothes, was still up reading when Trudy tapped lightly and stuck her head in the room to say good night.

"Charlotte and Ruby have gone to the movies together, but I haven't seen that Roy character all day," she informed them without their asking. "You don't think that Ruby will rub off on my Charlotte, do you? I was worried about the time she spent with Roy, but lately she's been with Ruby like they were joined at the hip. I just don't know what she sees in that hussy."

Trudy smiled. "Ruby's just as nice a person as Roy once you get to know her. I think it's wonderful that Charlotte has a friend so close to her own age. They probably have a lot in common."

"Yes, well, her old mother likes to see a movie once

in a while too," she said before going back to the pages of her book.

Listening from the hallway, Walker actually fought a sudden urge to walk into the room and give Helena a hug. She wouldn't appreciate his sympathy for her loneliness and the difficulty she was having in letting go of her daughter, but she wasn't such a bad old lady, he decided, warming to her from a distance.

As the night wore on, Trudy became quieter, more introspective, and very testy as her anxiety increased. Walker regretted having told her about their eavesdropper. There was no way of knowing how long he'd been listening or how long before he made his move. If Walker had kept the information to himself until George or Turner could discover the source, he might have been able to save her the mental anguish of waiting for something to happen.

Trudy's regular bedtime came and went. She felt drained but was wide awake and alert to every nuance in her immediate environment. She stayed close to Ian in the belief that two heads were better than one in a time of crisis, even though *he* grew quieter, more introspective, and very testy as the night wore on. He was an impatient man, battle-ready and eager to be done with it. He was also extremely concerned for her safety. She felt safe with him, but was growing weary of his mood.

"Why don't you go up to bed?" he suggested, tired of her pacing about the room. "You'll be the second person to know if anything starts to go down."

"Who'll be first?"

"Me!" He looked at her as if he thought she was incredibly stupid.

"Well, what if *I'm* the first to know? What if you fall asleep, and he sneaks in, cuts your throat, and then comes after me?" she suggested, hurt because he obviously thought she would be useless if the situation began to deteriorate.

"That's not the way it's going to happen," he said, trying to ease her rather dramatic imagination.

"The second floor is secure, and I'm going to be down here all night—awake. I'm not going to let anything happen to you."

"I'm hungry."

"Good. Why don't you get something to eat," he said, glad that she'd found a distraction.

"Don't you think it's sort of a strange time to be hungry? I'm not a nervous eater, you know. Do you suppose that they have the whole house bugged? They can do that now without ever entering the house. They have little radar things that they sit with in their cars and aim at the house, and they can hear every word that's said inside. I saw it on *Miami Vice* once."

"Do you really want me to answer all that?" he asked, staring at her as if she'd finally lost her mind.

"Why not? Is it so unreasonable to think that someone might be listening to every word we say?" she asked, indignant.

"Why the hell would they want to? I've been here for five days, and I haven't heard anything that made sense to me yet. If there was someone out there listening, they'd have turned the damned machine off by now." He stood and began to pace in the opposite direction from Trudy. "As to your being hungry, I can only guess the reason is that you haven't eaten anything all day. You slept through breakfast, and you played with your food at dinner. A possible solution would be a peanut butter sandwich."

Trudy had placed her hands on her hips during his tirade. She couldn't help it if she was a little nervous. People didn't try to break into her house and commit murder every day.

"Are you always this nasty when you work? It's not surprising that you had such an awful disposition when you first got here *or* that you work alone. I'm going to bed."

"Isn't that what I suggested in the first place? Or

are you hoping someone will sneak in and slit my throat?"

It was Trudy's turn to look as if he'd suddenly gone insane. "Why would I wish such a horrible thing?"

Why, indeed? he wondered as the air slowly leaked out of his lungs. What was the matter with him? What happened to all the comfort and support he wanted to give to her? After all she'd done for him, giving vent to his anger was a lousy way of repaying her.

"I'm sorry," he said. "I hate it when someone else is pulling all the strings, but I shouldn't have taken it out on you."

Her smile was small but forgiving. "I think we're both a little scared."

"I think we're both a lot scared. And tired. I have a great idea," he said, taking the steps that would enable him to put his arms around her.

"What is it?" she asked, smiling up into his face, feeling as if she belonged in his arms.

"You go up and get ready for bed, and I'll bring you a wonderful, wild, and woolly Walker deluxe sandwich—with mustard."

"Wow. That sounds wheelly ta-wific," she said, laughing. "But I'm going to have to take one of our famous rainchecks on it. I think I'd choke on anything I tried to eat right now."

"Are you sure? You need to eat."

"Maybe later."

"Try to get some sleep, then."

She nodded. By mutual, nonverbal consent they kept their good-night kiss light and easy. Both were very aware of the tenuous control they had over their emotions at the moment.

"Trudy?" He stopped her as she started up the stairs. She turned to look at him. "I don't think he's bugging anything but the phone. If he were going to get close enough to bug the house, he'd just come in and do the job. But he can use the phone to monitor any information—plane reservations, if you try to skip town, or appointments you make with your attorney in case you change your mind about the federal witness program—things like that."

Trudy smiled her appreciation. She hadn't expected him to go back and answer her question. He'd taken the time to do so just to calm her mind, and she loved him for that.

"It is two A.M.," the talking clock in the dining room announced loudly.

"Damn clock," Walker muttered, every nerve ending in his body standing straight on end. The clock had been declaring itself every half hour since Trudy had gone to bed. In the back of his mind he listened for it, prepared himself for it. But every time it spoke, it scared the holy living hell out of him.

He moved silently from room to room, checking locks on doors and windows, peering out to watch the shadows, waiting for one to move. A car would occasionally pass the house. Turner drove by twice every hour. But aside from the usual night noises, a rare sound from upstairs as someone rolled over in bed, and, of course, the clock, Walker heard nothing but his own breathing.

He tried to keep his mind a blank, an empty trap with which to catch anything unusual that came his way. But he found that disassociating himself was impossible. It wasn't like most of his other assignments. He'd always known the price he'd have to pay if he didn't succeed in his mission. But he wasn't willing to pay it this time.

He'd never *wanted* to die, but somehow it mattered more than ever before that he should live. He wanted to live. He wanted to grow to be a very old man someday—something he hadn't given much thought to before. Oh, he'd defend Trudy with his life when the time came. He had no doubt about that. He cared deeply for her. She was like a beacon of light shining bright on the moment, illuminating the possibility of a forever and nullifying the past by leaving it in total darkness. Without her he didn't seem to have a reason to want to grow old.

For the first time in years he saw himself living beyond the end of the assignment and the beginning of the next. He caught himself making plans and dreams. He felt enchanted by the idea of a baby and a mortgage and mowing the lawn. He had protected his right to have a home and family, but he'd neglected to claim them.

His future seemed endless. He wanted to fill it with love and laughter instead of lies and disaster. And he wanted Trudy with him to share it.

He carefully separated the folds in the dining room curtain and looked out into the dead of night as his head began to fill with thoughts of Trudy. She was the most important—

"It is two-thirty A.M."

The clock jerked his mind back to the present so fast, it caused him to act on reflex. His arm flew up, and his fist came barreling down through the center of the oblong box, smashing it into several nonspeaking pieces.

"Damn clock," he muttered, trying to feel remorse, wondering if he was going to have to replace it.

He was trying to decide which one of the several plausible explanations for the clock's demise he'd conjured up to give to Trudy in the morning, when he heard a vehicle rolling across the gravel in the alley at the back of the house.

Headlight beams rose up beyond the fence, the car stopped, and the lights went out. He couldn't see the car, but he knew that both Helena and Charlotte parked their cars at the rear of the house. Roy, who shared his car with Ruby, parked in front like Trudy.

A car door slammed shut, and then he didn't need to hear the banging of the gate or the clicking of heels on the walk to know that Charlotte and Ruby were home. Killers were usually more discreet and a little less conspicuous.

Not wanting to frighten them, he turned on the kitchen light and had a drink of water in his hand when he heard the key rattle in the lock of the back door.

"Hi," Charlotte said in a low, late-night voice. "What are you doing up so late?"

"The couch is lumpy. Where's Ruby?"

She looked nervous for a moment, and then she stammered, "Oh, I . . . we ran into Roy and he's bringing her home."

"Why?" He didn't care who came home with whom or why, but it did seem a little odd given the romantic link between her and Roy and the fact that she'd left with Ruby. If anything, she should have come home with one or the other of them and either the brother or sister should have come home alone. It was a natural question.

"Well, gee, I don't know. Let me think a minute. There would, of course, be a reason for that. . . ."

"A reason for what?" Roy asked, entering the kitchen from the front of the house.

Walker's hand was on his gun as he turned to face the man in the doorway. He was instantly furious that Roy had snuck up on him again. Both he and his sister moved around far too quietly, and it gave him the creeps. He didn't try to hide the fact either.

"Gotcha," Roy said, grinning as he walked over to the refrigerator and removed a can of beer. He offered one to both Charlotte and Walker, who shook their heads in refusal, and then he leaned against the counter to enjoy it. "So, what's happening?" he asked.

"Mr. Walker was here when I came in," Charlotte said, sounding innocent of any wrongdoing. "I was just on my way up to bed."

She beat a quick retreat from the room, hastily kissing Roy on the lips on her way out. Both men watched her go and then turned to stare at each other.

"You make her nervous," Roy said. "She's afraid you'll tell her mother about us."

"That's none of my business," Ian said, more of a reminder to himself than a word of comfort for Roy. He was developing a fondness for Helena that transcended her ugliness and domineering personality. He didn't feel that the young couple were being fair to the old lady, and that there might be a better way of handling their relationship than behind Helena's back—but it wasn't his problem. "What happened to your sister?"

"When?"

"Tonight," he said, running a hand through his hair impatiently. He stepped over to the sink beside Roy to rinse out his glass. "According to Charlotte, she came home with you. Where is she?"

Roy bent to look down the hallway from which he'd come, and then with an exaggerated frown of puzzlement said, "Gosh, I don't know. She was right behind me a second ago."

Walker gave him a vapid stare, trying hard to control his temper. He was ready to teach Roy a few things about life before restating his question, when he noticed what appeared to be makeup along the man's jaw, near his ear.

His eyes narrowed as he took a closer look at the man Roy and thought of the woman Ruby. There were so many similarities—the voice, the eyes, the coloring. Roy seemed a little taller than Ruby, but then again, he'd never allowed himself to get too close to her, either. He strained his brain trying to recall if he'd ever seen them together.

Musicians were onstage and under intense lighting, but did they wear makeup? He thought perhaps there was a chance that they might; however, his mind kept going back to review the likeness between the brother and sister, and to what George had told him over the phone the night before.

Catching the suspicion in Walker's expression and apparently reconsidering his sarcasm, Roy shrugged and admitted, "She was tired and feeling like a third wheel to Charlotte and me, so she went up to her room. Is something wrong?"

"No."

"You need to talk with her?"

Walker was tempted to say yes. He was beginning to suspect that there was more to the Roy/Ruby relationship than a mutual gene pool.

"No. Everything's fine. I'll just sleep easier knowing that everyone's in for the night," he said, moving away from Roy, acutely aware of his own masculinity.

He watched as Roy gave an indifferent shrug and tugged unconsciously on his shirt cuffs. "Well, sleep easy then," he said.

Walker listened until he heard a door close on the second floor before he let loose of the breath he'd been holding in his lungs. He liked to think of himself as a liberal, broad-minded sort of fellow who'd seen and learned to accept just about every social variation possible. Sexual freedom was something he believed in, it was a personal choice. But if what he'd guessed about Roy was true, it meant that Walker had been completely wrong about Ruby. The sensual, provocative, eat-'em-alive looks she'd been giving him and he'd been responding to began to give him the heebie-jeebies.

Could he have been so wrong about her? Shouldn't some innate part of his nature have alerted him to the possibility that Ruby wasn't equipped to carry out the heterosexual doings to which she'd constantly alluded? He rubbed his face briskly with his hands and smoothed back his hair before he turned out the light and walked back into the living room, shaking his head in bewilderment. What was happening to him?

From the moment he'd set eyes on Trudy in the park, it had been as if he were living in the twilight zone. People had been able to sneak up behind him whenever they wanted to; a frail woman had beat him nearly senseless; the *ugliest* woman in the world had found a soft spot in his heart; he'd fallen in love with a woman-child whom he couldn't seem to get into bed with on a sure-fire bet, and he hadn't been able to tell the difference between a man, a woman, and a transvestite. It was a nightmare, he decided even as he laughed softly in the early morning darkness.

"What's so funny?"

Walker's gun was half out of his shoulder holster before he recognized Trudy's voice. His eyes focused on the couch and soon distinguished her small form huddled on one end.

"I hope you're sleepwalking," he said, picking his way across the room in the darkness to join her.

"Why?" She snuggled beside him when his arm closed around her shoulders and he pulled her near.

"I'd hate to think you're really dumb enough to keep sneaking up on me the way you do. Your luck's going to run out on you one of these times, you know." His tone of voice was serious but not angry. He'd already concluded that a herd of elephants could rumble up behind him, and he wouldn't know it until one of them stepped on his head. It wasn't Trudy's fault that he was losing his edge. In fact, he was feeling a little sorry for her at the moment. Her cousin, George, had sent her one hell of a lousy bodyguard.

Reluctantly he admitted to himself that there was a possibility that George had been right in pulling him out of the field. Maybe he had played a few too many games. Perhaps his edge wasn't as sharp as it once had been. It might even be time for him to retire, he thought, not as shattered by the idea as he thought he would be.

"You won't shoot me. You'll stop yourself," she said, confident, breaking into his reverie. "And it's only temporary, you know. You're not going deaf. You just have a lot on your mind right now."

"Well, thanks for the information, Dr. Babbitt.

But it's not comforting. I'm supposed to be focused on keeping you alive."

"You will be when you need to be."

His chest vibrated as he chuckled at her sureness. It made his heart ache in a very good way to know she had such faith in him.

"Why are you up?" he asked, burying his face in her hair, letting the sweet scent of her fill his senses.

"I heard Roy and Charlotte . . . and Ruby come home. I didn't want to be alone anymore."

It registered in Walker's mind that Trudy was scared, but he chose to address her slight pause in mentioning Ruby rather than her fear.

"How well do you know Roy and Ruby?" he asked carefully, tuning into her answer for any indication that she might already know what he had just discovered. He wasn't sure how he was going to break the news to her if she didn't suspect anything.

"Pretty well. And they're not nearly as strange as Helena lets on."

"No? Have you ever seen the two of them together, at the same time?"

Her body was very still for a moment. "Ah. No. I can't say that I have. Why?"

"Don't you think that's a little strange."

She hesitated again. "No."

"Well, it is. It's very strange. They're brother and sister, living in the same house, and you never see them together? That's very strange."

"Are you trying to tell me something, Ian?"

He sighed, waiting for just the right words to come to him.

"Trudy, honey, I have reason to believe that Roy and Ruby are the same person."

"That's impossible. You can't be two people at once."

"No, I mean that I think Roy is a transvestite."

She giggled, sitting up to look at him as if she could see him in the darkness. "Oh, not you too.

Horace arrested poor Roy when he first figured ou[t] that Ruby wasn't real. But Roy doesn't for a momen[t] believe that he's Ruby. It's all an act. He imperson[n]ates all sorts of women. He does a wonderful Caro[l] Channing, and his Barbra Streisand is hilarious I've seen his act at the club. He's really wonderful.

"You knew? Why didn't you tell me?"

"It was a secret."

"What? A secret from whom? If it's part of his act who didn't know about it besides me? And why doe[s] he dress like that around here all day?" Walker wa[s] even more confused than before and feeling very pu[t] out about not having been told.

"It's a long, complicated story," she said, restin[g] her head on his chest once again. She wanted t[o] tell him everything, but the story wasn't hers to tell She could tell him only a few truths. "Roy put hi[s] costumes in Ruby's room to make it look like sh[e] lived here too. And he needed to be Ruby durin[g] the day to make it look like another person live[d] here. He chose Ruby, so he could be with Charlotte He couldn't very well dress up like Carol Channin[g] all day, you see, because that would have been to[o] obvious."

"For crying out loud. Why go to all that trouble[?] Why not just tell Helena and get it over with[?] They're going to have to tell her eventually."

Trudy said nothing. Silence had something to d[o] with discretion and valor, but it wasn't the same a[s] lying. She hadn't created the falsehood, but she wa[s] bound to uphold it until the bond was lifted. What ever conclusions Ian drew from what she told hi[m] were his own.

They sat in the silence together for several more minutes, brooding over the situation from opposite points of view.

"I have to admit that if it had been up to me,[']" she said, then yawned broadly and cuddled closer, "I don't think I would have made things quite so complicated. I've always found that lies are more believable if you keep them simple."

"That's true," he said, an authority on lies. He'd spent the past twelve years living one lie after another. "The simple and the obvious are always more difficult to detect. But I don't see the point in lying to Helena about their relationship. She'll find out the same way I did. And besides, the sooner she knows, the sooner she'll adjust to it."

"I thought the whole thing was pretty stupid, but it wasn't my decision to make." Trudy's voice was a groggy mumble.

By the time Walker was willing to confess that it wasn't any of his business either, Trudy was sound asleep on his chest.

He sighed contentedly and got comfortable. He held her like a baby and watched over her throughout the night. Baby-sitting had taken on a new meaning since the old days when he'd been saddled with his sisters, he decided as he looked down at Trudy's sweet face in the light of dawn. He closed his eyes as he tried to commit her image to memory.

He saw a picture of her in his mind but knew intuitively that it wasn't Trudy he was seeing. It was his daughter. She was beautiful and full of grace and happiness. He felt pride swell in his chest. He sensed a devotion to the child that was greater than any he'd ever had for anything else in the world, a bond that went far beyond the human condition to something supernatural. And yet, with such powerful emotions coursing through his veins, he knew in his heart that the child's greatest significance to him was what she represented. She was the product of the love he felt for Trudy.

"How long are we going to have to pussyfoot around here, anyway?" Helena asked. It was mid-morning and her television game shows were about to begin. She stood frowning down at Ian as he slept with his neck and shoulders bent into one corner of the couch. "He hasn't moved a muscle in hours. He'll feel like a pretzel when he wakes up."

"He must have been very tired," Trudy whispered back, grimacing at the contorted position he'd assumed. "Didn't you hear him prowling around all night?"

"Was that before or after he killed the clock?"

Trudy chuckled as she pictured the event, but she did so quietly. She didn't relish the idea of waking Ian up. He was going to be very angry with himself for having fallen asleep. How he expected to stay awake for twenty-four hours a day, for however long it took the killer to make a move, was beyond her. A man needed to sleep, and now was as good a time as any in her opinion.

Seconds later the matter was taken out of her hands altogether when the phone rang. Ian was instantly awake.

"What the hell is that?" he roared, disoriented and out of sorts. He came off the couch with his neck bent at a forty-five-degree angle.

"Relax. If you murder the phone, I might as well not even bother watching the home shopper network today," Helena said, a severe warning in her voice.

"I'll get it," Trudy said, dashing away.

"Trudy?" The familiar voice on the other end of the line sent a cold chill up Trudy's spine.

"George?"

"I checked out Sophie Williams. They did have her registered at the Creek of Peace Nursing Home, up until two days ago," he said.

"I know. Horace already told us."

"Then you know she's dead."

"Who?"

"Sophie Williams. She died two days ago at the nursing home."

"But Horace was told last night that she wasn't taking any calls."

"It would be difficult for her," he said, his humor as dry as toast. "I got the same message, actually, but I went over the receptionist's head to the director. He said they were having some difficulty notifying Sophie's family of her death and didn't want the news released until after they'd been contacted."

"So . . ."

"So you know what to tell Walker, don't you?"

"Yes."

"You okay?"

"Yes. I just thought there would be more time."

"There'll be more time when it's over, Trudy. Take care," he said, and then the line went dead.

She held the phone in both hands for a long moment before she could bring herself to hang up. Time would go on only for those who survived what was about to happen, she thought. Her hands shook, and it became more and more difficult to breathe as George's words took their full effect. Her throat was so tight.

Time. Time. She wanted more time. There were so many things she still needed to do. So many things she hadn't told Ian as yet. So many things she wanted to give him. She had to have more time, but she didn't think Sophie was going to understand or cooperate with her.

Sophie. Trudy's mind clamped down on the short, aged person who was not Sophie Williams at all but a ruthless killer who would murder anyone for a price. Then she thought of Ian.

From deep within her, her well-known urge to run and hide began to bubble and churn. She and Ian should get in the car, turn on the ignition, and disappear, she told herself. They should lose themselves so completely, no one could find them. No government, no powerful individual, no one. But it was too late.

Ian would never back away once he knew who the assassin was. He'd feel obliged to stay and eliminate the threat. He'd do that, thinking he was protecting her. No, Ian would never run away. And she could never leave him behind.

Don't panic. Don't panic. Think calmly and rationally, she told herself over and over again until at last what had to be done became as clear as the air she was breathing. At that same moment she was jolted by the impact of just how much Ian had come to mean to her. He hadn't come into her world to protect her, he'd come to *be* her world. If anything happened to him, it would happen to her as well.

A cloud of euphoria seemed to settle about her. She knew she wouldn't run away. And she knew she wouldn't let anything happen to Ian. Part of her was still terrified and trembling with cowardice, but at the moment the rest of her felt like a brave, courageous warrior. She could only pray that the one would continue to suppress the other until she could accomplish the most important mission in her life.

"Who was on the phone?" Ian asked, coming into the kitchen a short time later.

"George," she said in a dull, absent tone of voice, her thoughts elsewhere.

"What's wrong? What did he say?" The look on Trudy's face was heart-stopping. Her eyes had a vacant, faraway look to them, and the roses had been washed from her cheeks. She looked . . . dazed.

"He's dead."

"Who's dead?"

"Claude Packston," she said, forcing herself to look him straight in the eye.

"Are you sure?"

"Call George and see," she said, moving away from the phone, pretending she had nothing to hide.

"But how? When?"

"He's dead, Ian. It's over. It's really over," she said, smoothly avoiding the necessity of telling another lie. To make her ploy all the more believable, she was going to have to act excited, she decided.

She threw herself into his arms—a not-so-difficult ask—and forced a smile to her lips.

"I'm so excited," she said, mentioning her condition so that he would notice it and perhaps play long with her. For a note of reality, she added, "I ust can't believe it."

"Me either. It doesn't seem possible." He was rowning as he held her. His hands moved up and lown her back in a soothing, protective fashion. He vas having a hard time accepting the fact that she vas safe. Something just didn't feel right to him.

"But it is. I promise you it is," she said. "Let's go ell the others."

Walker glanced at the phone as he followed her ut of the room. The seed of doubt in his brain was aking root and growing rapidly. Why hadn't George isked to talk to him? Where were all the specifics? "he how, the where, the why that George would ave gone into great detail about? And what about he wiretap?

How well did Trudy know her cousin George? How amiliar was she with his voice and his manner of ipeaking? Would she be able to tell the difference ietween George and someone who merely said he vas George?

He prodded his feet to walk past the phone. He'd et Trudy have this moment of peace because she ooked so happy. But Walker planned to call his pal George at the earliest opportunity and get all the iews firsthand.

"Can you believe it, Helena? It's over. There won't ie anyone coming to kill me after all," Trudy was iaying as Walker entered the room.

"You sound disappointed," Helena said, hardly ooking up from her program.

Chowder, sleeping at his master's feet, opened one ye, gave Trudy a bored stare, and went back to ileep.

"Well, I didn't think Mr. Packston would send any-ine to kill me in the first place. It's a little hard to

get overwhelmed with pleasure when you find ou
something you didn't think was going to happe
isn't going to happen," she said. Would that expla
nation cover the fluctuations in her behavior? sh
wondered. Maintaining a facade of great happines
when there was nothing to be happy about wa
harder than she thought it would be. "He's dead
you know. I can't be happy about that," she adde
for good measure.

Having delivered the news to Helena, and gotte
very little support in doing so, Trudy was glad of th
response she received from Charlotte and Rub
when they returned home from a shopping trip a
lunchtime.

"How wonderful," Charlotte said, hugging Trudy
"Now you'll be able to get on with your life in a
close to a normal fashion as possible. I'm so happ
for you, Trudy."

"I suppose that means that Mr. Tall, Dark, an
Handsome will be leaving soon, huh?" Ruby asked
looking down at Ian, who was seated at the kitche
table. She winked broadly at him, and when h
glowered back at her, she blew him a loud kiss.

Trudy, seeing the exchange, giggled. "Careful
Ruby, he knows," she said.

Ruby didn't bat an eye but continued to smile a
Ian in an extremely licentious manner. Ian release
a long-suffering sigh and turned his attention bac
to the sardine sandwich Trudy had insisted on mak
ing him for lunch. In light of the way he felt abou
Ruby, the meal was taking on some appeal.

"We're taking Mother over to the club this after
noon to rehearse something special. Would you lik
to come and watch?" Charlotte asked Trudy, extend
ing the invitation to Walker with her friendly smile
"We're going to try to work Ruby into our magi
act."

Walker gasped in disbelief, and then choked a
one of the sardines slithered down his throat. H
coughed and sputtered as Trudy aimlessly struck

low after blow to his back, saying, "What a marvelous idea. Just Ruby or Bette Davis too. I love it hen you're Bette Davis. Does Helena know about his?"

"Mother thinks that as long as we're spending so uch time together, Ruby should learn an honest ade," Charlotte said with a secretive smile. "She aid Ruby could learn the tricks that required cramming herself into small places. She says they mess p her hair, but the truth is, she just doesn't fit nto small places anymore."

Trudy laughed. "Well, I hate to miss it, but I think m going to take a nap this afternoon. I didn't sleep ery well last night, and I'm exhausted."

"Me too," Walker said, and then as everyone in the oom gave him a knowing look, he added, "The ouch is lumpy and there were people coming and oing all night long."

"We understand," Ruby said, smiling her smile hat could curl a man's hair. She wagged her delicate brows at Walker, who ground his teeth together ard.

Sophie shuffled into the room and was greeted indly by all—including Trudy, who was still gathering up the courage she would need to carry out her ask of love. To act less than friendly toward Sophie vould appear peculiar.

"Would you like me to make you a sardine sandwich, Sophie? I have a few left here in the can," rudy said, schooling her features as best she could.

"Ah. No, thank you, dear. Fish upsets my stomch," Sophie replied, eyeing Walker's meal with uckered lips. She took a free chair at the table, dug leep into her bag for her knitting, and set to clicking her sticks slowly.

Charlotte invited Sophie to join them for the afternoon, but the old woman declined, claiming that he tired easily.

It wasn't long before mother, daughter, and . . . riend took their leave. It was the moment Trudy

had been waiting for. She was pretty sure th
Sophie wasn't being paid to murder everyone in th
house and was simply waiting to catch her victi
alone before carrying out her foul deed.

Trudy knew what she needed to do next to kee
Ian out of harm's way. A good excuse to lure herse
away from the house without him would set thing
into motion.

Ten

"You know, I think I'm too exhausted to sleep," Trudy said, scratching behind Chowder's ear as he lay on her lap. "My body's tired, but my mind just keeps grinding away."

"Would a back rub help?" Ian asked. Fortunately his voice contained only sympathy and understanding, because her true heart's desire was to take him upstairs and make slow, sweet love before falling asleep in his arms. The slightest bit of encouragement from him might have been her undoing. And she had no doubt that if they put themselves in a vulnerable position, Sophie would take the opportunity and kill them both.

As it was, her mind remained set on a higher mission—saving Ian's life. She smiled her love and gratitude to him, and then set Chowder on the floor.

"You're sweet to offer, but why don't you go ahead and try to get some sleep yourself? I think I want to go for a walk. Maybe it'll clear my mind a little."

"I'll go with you."

"Thanks, but I haven't been truly alone for months now. Would you mind awfully if I went by myself this time?"

"Yes, I would mind," he said emphatically. "It may be over for Packston, but we don't know that his hit man has heard the news about his death yet. He could still be out there."

"He's not. George would have said so when he called," she argued. The stubborn expression on Ian's face didn't waver. "I won't go far. I promise. And I'll take Chowder with me."

"Not for protection, I hope." He gave the sleeping moplike dog a derisive look. "He couldn't fight his way out of a paper bag."

"So you know he's not going to want to walk very far, either," she said, smiling persuasively. "Just down to the park and back. Please."

Well, if he put a call in to George the minute she left, he could be with her in a few minutes if he didn't get an all clear, he calculated. Then, too, just looking at her made it almost impossible for him to deny her anything.

"Okay. But if you're not back in ten minutes, I'll come after you," he said against his better judgment. If it were up to him, he wouldn't ever let her out of his sight, danger or no danger.

He stood on the porch and watched her walk down the block until she was out of sight. He calculated the remaining minutes it would take her to drag Chowder to the park and back again, and figured he'd have just enough time to call George and get all his questions answered.

He stepped back into the house to find Sophie seated in an overstuffed chair with her knitting in her lap.

"Where has our little Trudy gone?" she asked, turning her pruny mouth into a wrinkled smile.

"For a short walk. She'll be right back," he said, eager to get to the phone. "If you'll excuse me, I need to make a phone call."

"Certainly, dear. You just go on about your business. I don't want to be a bother to anyone."

"You're no bother, Sophie. I'll be only a minute."

"I'll be fine, dear. Don't you worry."

Walker hurried into the kitchen and picked up the

hone. He'd dialed two numbers before something ard and deadly was rammed into his ribs near his pine.

"Hang it up, Walker," a high-pitched and sinister oice ordered him from behind. "The only person vho wants to talk to you is me. I have a message to leliver, and I don't have a lot of time to do it. So lang it up. Now."

Walker was caught off guard and confused, but is recovery time was as instantaneous as it ever lad been. In a push-button reaction, his emotions lutomatically shut down, his thought processes lecame razor-sharp, and by reflex he was as cold lnd calculating as any machine.

As he slowly lowered the receiver onto its cradle, lis mind raced through his options. Escaping never lntered the picture, although he was acutely aware lf the three entrances leading into the kitchen from le dining room, the hall, and the backyard as pos- lible distractions to his attacker. Instead, he zeroed l n on neutralizing his would-be assassin—and doing lt before Trudy walked into the middle of something lhat he instinctively knew had nothing to do with ler.

With his hands at shoulder level, he carefully lturned to face his adversary. Under normal circum- stances Walker might have been surprised to see Sophie Williams with a gun aimed at his chest, but as it was, he merely stood quietly and studied her closely—her stance, her height, weight, and the way she held her revolver.

"Slowly place your weapon inside the refrigerator, please," she said, her voice heartier than the soft, breathless tones she usually spoke in. Walker com- plied in slow motion.

"You have led me a merry chase these past four months, Mr. Walker. I was beginning to think you had once again left your country to meddle in affairs that are none of your concern," Sophie said, more confident now that Walker was disarmed. "My

employer is most eager that you do not return to hi
country anytime in the future."

"Yerkovich?" Walker asked, as curious as he wa
eager to distract the woman by talking to her.

Mr. Yerkovich had been a rather large feather in
his cap several years earlier, who had sworn to do
some rather nasty work on his anatomy before wip
ing him off the face of the earth. He was also one o
the few men he knew with enough connections in
the American government to be able to track him
on his own turf.

"No. But I'm sure that gentleman will be eternally
indebted to Señor Quintero for his ingenuity and
proficiency in engaging me to deal with your abomi
nable behavior of late," she said.

"Quintero's missing his coca plants, huh?"
Walker said, smiling. He shrugged. "Fires happen
Hell, I'll bet that by the time he gets out of prison
twenty or thirty years from now, those fields'll be
ready for replanting. He can go right back into busi
ness if he still wants to. So, you see, this is totally
unnecessary."

"I'm afraid he's not as amused by the incident as
you appear to be, Mr. Walker."

"Well, he probably thinks I had something to do
with the Colombian government confiscating every
thing he owns, but that's not the case. They
arrested him. I just put him and a couple of his
Peruvian buddies out of business."

"He claims he once trusted you," she said with
disapproval ringing in her voice. She apparently
believed in the myth about honor among thieves.

"That was his problem, not mine. I didn't trust
him any further than I could have thrown him."

"Well, apparently you underestimated the dis
tance, Mr. Walker. You should have known he'd
send someone after you."

"Which brings us to you, I guess," Walker said
evenly, speculating on the time and distance between
him and the gun. "Do you have a name?"

"It's Methuselah," Trudy said, stepping into the kitchen from the dining room, looking as cool and collected and out of place as a Mafia moll in church. She dropped Chowder's leash at the door and approached them from the side, walking slowly and unthreateningly.

Chowder started to follow her but was overcome with fatigue halfway across the room. He fell like a throw pillow in the middle of the floor and went fast asleep.

The woman's eyes darted in Trudy's direction, but only for an instant. Her gun never wavered. She was single-minded in her intent and obviously considered Trudy's presence a triviality.

Walker, on the other hand, thought he might explode as all the emotions he'd suppressed came gushing to the surface of his consciousness with terror and rage leading the way. His throat constricted into a tight knot, and he held his breath as he watched Trudy advance toward him.

"Ah, Trudy. You should've run. Why didn't you run?" he asked with pain and sorrow in his voice. He felt sick inside.

She reached up and cupped his face with the palm of her hand, and then she grinned at him. "What? And leave you here to die alone? Never."

She let her eyes tell Ian of her love, and then she finally looked away when Ian kept staring at her as if she had, at last, gone mad. She had work to do.

"It is Methuselah, isn't it?" she asked, looking back to the old woman, watching her intently. "I mean, when you're not pretending to be some poor dead person from a nursing home?"

"How do you know that, dear Trudy?" she asked, her eyes narrowing slightly, her voice growing tight with suspicion.

"Oh, I know lots of things," she said. She then turned her head and smiled at Ian. "Can you believe this? Such a sweet little ol' lady, a common cut-throat. What's the world coming to?"

Walker didn't get the chance to answer her. The woman's sharp voice cut the air like a rapier as she repeated her question. "I asked you how you knew my name?"

"Well, I don't know your real name. I just know that you use the name Methuselah when someone wants to hire you to commit murder. At first we thought it was because you were rather old when you started to kill professionally, but I also think you were trying to make us think you were a man. I know Interpol will be interested in hearing you're a woman." She paused briefly before adding, "Either way, it's a clever name. Very catchy. And murder's got to pay better than social security."

"Very amusing, dear girl. But I'm still waiting to hear how you got your information."

"Well, it's kind of a long story," she said, sidestepping a short distance away from Ian. "Do we have the time?"

The woman shifted her weight and her gun in Trudy's direction. Nothing was said. She merely glared with the most evil-looking eyes Trudy had ever seen.

Swallowing convulsively, she took a deep breath to maintain her calm. She'd come too far to let her cowardly heart get the best of her now, she decided, refusing to think of anything but the moment.

Walker thought he might die waiting for Trudy to start talking again. He held his breath, knowing that if she was going to go into one of her explanations, his chance to act would come when the woman's head was spinning in circles.

"Well, it seems that Ian's friend, Mr. Quintero, has a very nosy cellmate, who, it seems, is also a very crafty fellow. He traded some information he overheard for an early release. The Colombian government, who very much appreciated Ian's endeavors against their favorite drug lord on their behalf, sent word to my cousin George, who also happens to be a very good friend of Ian's." She stopped speaking ong enough to take a deep breath, and then she continued. "Now, my cousin George can be an extremely irritating man, but he knows people. And he knows Ian especially well. He knew that Ian would do nothing to protect himself from you. He would have simply taken his chances with you, when you showed up to kill him. And under normal circumstances, George might have accepted this decision, because he thinks Ian is the best there is. But Ian's been through some rough times lately, and he hasn't been functioning at peak level. You might have noticed this . . . well, maybe not, since you don't know Ian all that well. Anyway, George was worried and thought he might need a little help this time. So we lured him here and we've been waiting for you to follow him. And that's how I know who you are."

With her story at an end, she looked from one to the other and found them both staring at her as if she'd suddenly turned green and grown fangs.

It was Ian who reacted first. With pain in his eyes and a voice lower than any she'd ever heard him use, he uttered, "It was all a setup?"

"No," she said, responding instantly to the agony she saw in his expression. He was feeling betrayed— not by George but by her and all they'd shared in the short time they'd been together. "Ian. What you're thinking is wrong."

All at once it was as if a metal visor fell in front of his face, blocking his thoughts and emotions from her view. He shut her out of his life and looked as dark and angry as he had the first time she'd seen him.

That hurt. She was trying to save his life and was very likely going to die in the process, and *he* was mad? Not a person to anger easily, Trudy sighed with impatience. How could he possibly believe that she would betray him or think that she could pre- tend to care for him when she didn't? What kind of

person did he think she was? The more she though
about it, the more annoyed she became.

"Don't worry, Trudy," Methuselah said after some
quiet contemplation of her own, "Mr. Walker wil
soon realize that what you have said isn't completely
true. I'm sure it will be too late for him by then, bu
. . . well, you did your best."

"What's that supposed to mean?" she asked, too
annoyed to be afraid.

"Well, if this was a setup to capture me, where
is your great American cavalry that always comes
dashing to the rescue at the last minute?"

"Well, to tell you the truth, I don't know," she said
finding yet another reason to be perturbed. "I was
supposed to come in here, assess the situation, and
say your name—which was the code word for them
to charge in. I don't mind telling you that I'm a little
disappointed."

She looked at Ian then, and giving him a look
he couldn't possibly misconstrue, she said, "I think
we're going to handle this on our own, Ian."

She took another baby step away from Ian to draw
Methuselah's attention.

"Don't be stupid," the woman said, motioning her
back toward Walker with the gun.

Then she aimed it once again at Ian's chest, forc
ing Trudy to comply. But before she could reach his
side, all hell broke loose in the kitchen.

With her usual grace, Trudy tripped over her own
feet and fell sideways toward Walker. Methuselah
instinctively took a defensive step backward, her
finger tightening around the trigger of the gun as
a piercing yowl rose up from Chowder, whose tai
Methuselah was standing on. Like a lightning bolt,
the dog shot through the air and sunk his teeth
deep into the old woman's fleshy posterior. In her
pain, she bent double with her arm extended, firing
her gun into the floor. And in the time it took
Walker to leap over Trudy to grab Methuselah's fore-

rm and break it over his knee to release the gun,
here were five guns pointed at Methuselah.

Dazed, Walker stepped away from the writhing
body on the floor and looked around in confusion.
There stood Roy, Charlotte, Helena, and Horace
Turner in various stages of readiness, their guns
drawn and cocked. George was putting his pistol
back into the holster on his belt.

Some of Walker's numbness was wearing off, and
he was about to demand an explanation from
George, when he glanced at Trudy. His stinging
words froze on his lips at the sight of the expression
on her face.

Trudy was on her feet—and spitting mad. She
took two steps forward and with all her might threw
her fist into George's midsection. His groan of pain
brought her very little satisfaction.

"Where were you?" she demanded in a voice filled
with as much hysteria as anger. "You said this
wouldn't happen. You said it wouldn't be anything
like last time. You said you'd follow me in and jump
her the second I gave the word. I talked until I was
blue in the face, George. Where were you? You could
have gotten Ian killed. You could have gotten us
both killed. As far as I'm concerned, we're even. My
debt is paid. So don't you ever ask me to do anything like this again. Understand?"

George groaned again and nodded several times.

"What debt? What the hell is going on here?"
Walker finally bellowed, angry, resentful, and hurt.
"This is my life you people are playing with here.
I'm the one who was manipulated and lied to. If
anyone has a right to be mad, it's me."

"Oh, shut up, Ian," Trudy shouted back, turning
to face him. She was trembling from the inside out
and realized that most of her fury was the aftermath
of the most frightening moments of her life. She'd
come so close to losing Ian forever that she couldn't
bear to think of it. Instead, she was uncontrollably
angry.

"Don't even think about starting that garbage with me, Ian Walker. You have absolutely no right to be angry, because we haven't been *playing* with your life. In case you hadn't noticed yet, we just saved it for you. And you haven't been any more manipulated than the rest of us. None of us was particularly thrilled with the idea of this, but for one reason or another, it seems we were all in debt to George." She cast the man a withering glance. "He's the one who thought you were worth saving from this murdering maniac. The rest of us had no idea who you were when this was all set up. We were only paying off favors, just like you."

"But if it's truth you want," she ranted, hardly taking a second breath, "I can give you the truth. I don't know what each of us owed George for because I never thought it was any of my business. But Helena is a retired Secret Service agent"—she looked at the woman and couldn't help smiling—"who's been having the time of her life because she owns a stationery store now and it bores her to death."

Trudy could feel some of her ire slipping away as she thought of how close they'd all become in the past few weeks while waiting for and then watching over Ian. She looked to Charlotte and Roy and continued to speak in a gentler tone of voice.

"Roy and Charlotte are married. They were both police officers in Washington, D.C., once, and I know that Roy worked undercover for a long time and that Charlotte was with narcotics for a while. They have two daughters that they haven't seen in weeks because of what they owed George. And I suspect that he's been holding their voucher for a while because he needed Roy to act as two people, so we'd have the correct number of boarders in case inquiries were made. Roy not only impersonates women, he does men as well. He's a wonderful impersonator, although I don't know why George wanted us to tell you that elaborate lie about Helena being Charlotte's

nother and all. I think that was just to keep your
mind occupied so you wouldn't pick up on what we
were doing."

She sighed then, most of her anger spent. There
was only one explanation left to make. Hers. And
she was afraid of what Ian might think of her once
she told her story.

Stalling for time, she glanced down at the old
woman on the floor. She didn't look too deadly anymore. She looked weak and frail . . . like Sophie.

Trudy caught a look in Charlotte's eyes that asked
if she wanted the room cleared so she could be alone
with Ian. She shook her head, filled her lungs with
air and her soul with courage, then looked back to
finish what she'd started with Ian.

"I'm not ashamed of anything I've done," she said,
her head held high. "I told you what happened when
I ran away from my parents, but what I didn't tell
you was that I spent the rest of my life trying to
prove to myself that I wasn't a coward. Sometimes
I wonder if I wasn't trying to kill myself, but at the
time I wasn't thinking of it in that way. I just had
to do everything that frightened me the most, prove
how brave I was.

"I did a lot of crazy things as a kid that almost
drove my grandparents to drink, but it wasn't until
I took a job with the Justice Department and got
involved with a task force against organized crime
that I really got a chance to show my true colors.
After a while I began to think that maybe I wasn't
so bad, or maybe I just started growing up. I don't
know. I was still afraid, and I felt cowardly inside,
but somehow it didn't seem to be such a bad thing.
I knew that if I cared enough about something that
I'd fight for it, I wouldn't run away." She eased her
weight from one foot to the other and stuck her
hands in her pockets as the story became more
uncomfortable in its telling. "Two years ago I . . . I
had to kill a man. He was a creep, and I did it in self-
defense, but I . . . I didn't like killing him. I hated it.

I . . . there was no way I could justify killing people even scum, to prove that I was a worthy person George got me off the task force and destroyed my files so I couldn't be traced."

She'd been watching Ian's unreadable face throughout her dissertation. He revealed nothing No scorn. No compassion. Nothing. She waited for his comment on what she'd just told him, but he just stood there staring at her, unblinking. Suddenly, with her anger and fear dissipated, she felt hollow inside. All she had left was an enormous love for a man who felt she'd betrayed him, and the guilt of knowing that she had, no matter how justified the cause.

Ian was a proud man. He'd told her things about his life that she knew he'd never told to another living soul. He was a brave man who was used to being the protector not the protected. Was he feeling shame and embarrassment because they had conspired to save his life? What was he thinking? What was he feeling? Trudy knew she couldn't make him tell her. She couldn't help him if he wouldn't talk to her. She decided to take one last shot at getting through to him, and then it would be up to him.

"If you can honestly say that you had your head screwed on straight when you came home from Colombia and that you could have handled this attempt on your life in a calm, rational, and reasonable fashion, then I think . . ." All at once she felt like crying. She kept picturing him walking out of her life. There was a rocklike lump in her throat, and she could feel her chin begin to quiver. She fought to control it, even as it threatened to overwhelm her. "I think you should tell us so that we can apologize for our parts in this scheme and kill George for putting us to all this trouble. But if you can't honestly say that, then there's just one last thing I'm going to say."

"Trudy," he said, but she held up a hand to stop him.

"Those were my grandparents you spoke to and this is my house. My boarders have been living at the hotel in town for weeks now. There really was a Claude Packston, and he really did try to kill me after I testified against him before the grand jury. The lies that we told you were George's idea, but they were also for your protection. And you've been told a lot of truths too." She took a wild swipe at a rogue tear that had escaped her blurring eyes to roll down her cheek. "I wasn't lying when I told you that I love you, and I'm not going to beg you to forgive me for saving your life. I'm going to go upstairs, and if you'd like to come up and make love for the rest of our lives, well"—the tears were rolling freely and unchecked in the turmoil of emotion she was feeling—"that would make me very happy. But if you hate me for what I've done, then . . . well, then I think you should leave with George."

With that she reached down the front of her shirt and yanked, pulling out a small wireless transmitter. Then she reached behind her and removed a cold, brutal-looking knife from the waistband of her jeans.

"Good-bye, George," she said softly, placing both the device and the knife into his hands. "Say hi to Aunt Milly for me, will you?"

Walker was two steps behind Trudy as she walked out of the room and was about to scoop her into his arms, never to let her go again, when Helena stopped him. She grabbed his forearm as he marched by her, jerking him around in the doorway.

"Why don't you give her a couple of minutes to pull herself together?" she said, her ugly old face smiling at him kindly.

"I don't want her to think that I don't love her. Not for a second," he said, voicing his greatest fear.

"She knows." When Walker hesitated to believe her, she explained. "This was hard for her in the first place. Falling in love with you made it all the worse. She was afraid she was going to have to kill old Methuselah here, and she came too close to losing you. All in all, it's not been a great day for her."

The understatement released an incredulous laugh from Walker. "Well, at least now I know how to get her to answer me, straight and to the point." He leaned against the doorjamb and shook his head in awe. "Wasn't she great? Did you see how mad she was?"

The door at the end of the hall was closed as Walker approached it. He listened outside and could hear Trudy moving about inside, but couldn't make out whether or not she was still crying. He hoped she wasn't. He knew he should have said something to her earlier, but he honestly thought she was lying at first and couldn't understand why. Then, when the others corroborated her tale with their silence, it seemed too unreal to believe. It wasn't until she'd said that she loved him and indicated that she thought he might hate her that the enormity of what they had done, what she had done, finally sank in through the confusion. And for a brief moment he hadn't known what to say. Thank you seemed a little lame in light of all they'd sacrificed for him, a total stranger.

The doorknob rattled in his hand as he turned it, alerting Trudy to his presence. She turned to face him as he entered. Standing on the far side of the bed in a short white chemise with little red spots on it, she looked nervous and regal at once. The expression on her face told him that she was eager to see him but that she wasn't going to grovel or beg him to stay. He couldn't imagine loving her more than he did at that moment. She had so much heart in such a small body.

Trudy had saved more than just the flesh and blood of his life. With her innate goodness and the innocence of her love, she'd snatched his spirit from he jaws of death and breathed life back into his oul.

He stepped into the room and leaned back on the loor to close it, all the while wondering if he'd ever ire of looking at her.

"You look as if you were pretty sure that I'd come up here," he said, more amused than accusing.

She gave a slight shake of her head and stepped o the end of the bed. She'd never been more unsure of anything in her life.

"Only hopeful," she said, her entire being aching profoundly with her need to know his thoughts and eelings.

She stood with her arms at her sides, making it lear to Walker that she had gone as far as she ould. If he wanted her, he was going to have to go o her.

Well, he wanted her, he admitted without reservaion as he pushed himself away from the door and valked across the room toward her.

"That's a nice touch," he said, casually glancing at the dozen or so candles placed on the tables and shelves around the bed. He reached out to turn off he lamp on the vanity and slowly turned to face ner. "On top of everything else, you're romantic."

"I wanted our first time to be special. It's not as f it's happening recklessly or spontaneously, so I hought—" she broke off self-consciously and gave a helpless little shrug.

"I don't know. I'm feeling a little reckless right now. You're a lot more than I'd bargained for, Trudy."

"You mean . . . because of what I was, what I used o do? I don't do that anymore. My life is very quiet now, and I'm very ordinary."

He chuckled, closed the short distance between hem, and laid his hands on her hips. "Baby, you couldn't be ordinary to save your soul. And I don't give a damn about your past. All I care about is now and tomorrow."

Trudy's shuddering sigh of relief seemed to com
all the way up her body from her toes. His blac
eyes held her motionless, or she surely would hav
fallen to the floor in a heap as the tension draine
out of her.

"I kept hearing the front door closing, and
thought . . . I thought you'd . . ."

"You thought I'd left," he said, adoring her fac
with his gaze. In her eyes he saw his destiny, hi
joy, and all the contentment he could hope for i
his life. "They took Methuselah and left. We're alon
in the house."

Alone? Did that matter? she wondered throug
the haze clouding her mind. She felt numb excep
for the warmth of Ian's hands on her hips. She wa
fairly certain that she was no longer breathing, an
her heart was an erratic annoyance that would sud
denly stop or beat in her throat or low in her ches
at inconsistent intervals. She felt lost to the world
finding her only reality in Ian's face, in the touch o
his hands.

"George told me about Claude Packston," sh
heard him say in a soft, concerned voice. "You reall
did walk in on him after he'd killed his wife. H
killed the two cops guarding you after you testifie
to the grand jury, and then he turned the gun o
you."

"I had to kill him," she whispered, unaware of an
regret she might be feeling. All she wanted was fo
Ian to kiss her. All she could think of was the fee
of his hands on her body.

Ian's left hand came up and slipped the strap o
her chemise from her shoulder. His fingers light
caressed her, then moved lower until they found th
scar on her back.

"This is where he shot you, isn't it?" he asked
His voice had a harsh, rasping quality to it.

She nodded. "I was afraid it would happen all ove
again today," she uttered.

He turned her slightly to the side to get a bette

ook at the scar, to run a finger along the pink-
inged ridge of tissue from top to bottom. His dark
ead bent over her pale shoulder, and he dropped
weet, healing kisses to her old wound.

She closed her eyes and tried to swallow. Her body
rickled with need. She grew weak under his gentle
ministry.

When he was finished, he turned her face in his
lirection to get her attention. Her eyes remained
losed, her thoughts her own, and he felt an
urgency grip him. Was she recalling the pain and
uffering she'd endured at the hands of Claude
ackston? How could he help her? What could he
lo to ease her conscience? His hand slid down her
eck and across her throat. He felt her heart beating
gainst his palm as he passed it over her soft
leavage.

A smile quirked his lips as he noticed for the first
ime that the little red spots on her short nightie
vere actually small hearts—another example that
he was all woman with the heart of a child.

He continued to trace the outline of her breasts
long the low neckline of the garment but pulled her
loser, saying, "Look at me, Trudy."

When she obeyed, he smiled at her. What he had
magined she was thinking was quite obviously the
ast thing on her mind. The passion and desire in
er eyes nearly bowled him over, but it also thrilled
im beyond anything he'd ever known before.

"Trudy Babbitt, I love you." He took her lower lip
between his teeth and tugged gently, teasing a
response from her. She opened her mouth and
eather-touched her lips to his over and over. He
lamped his mouth over hers and ravished her with
is tongue. He tickled and cajoled, deepening the
kiss and their passion until they were both groping
or the bed.

Trudy felt the buttons on Ian's shirt give way and
got a little heady with her newfound strength. She
bushed the material off his shoulders, craving his

warmth and the feel of his flesh. Her mind reeled
She felt his hands on her thighs as they move
upward under the soft cotton of her chemise. Sh
pressed his buttocks closer, writhed as her torture
emotions sought a release. Her breath came i
gasps; her heart pounded in her ears.

Walker was on fire. He burned to possess her, t
hear her scream in ecstasy, and to take his ow
pleasure in her body. The flame inside him was ho
and bright. He could hear it snapping and sizzling
He could smell the smoke.

He jerked his head away from the hard tip of Tru
dy's breast. Something was wrong. *He really di*
smell smoke!

He spun around like one of Trudy's toys until h
caught sight of the blaze of fire crawling up the cur
tain beside the bed. In a flash he was off the be
and ripping the curtain down from the wall. In on
motion he grabbed a pillow and threw the curtai
to the floor, and there he smothered it to death.

Walker slowly got to his feet, weak from the sigh
of the destruction on the floor and aghast at how
close it had come to consuming them. He staggere
a little as he tried to control his rapid breathing an
the racing of his heart.

"Oh no," he heard Trudy wail. He looked at he
and saw tears welling in her eyes. "We're doomed,
she cried. "We'll never make love. You were right al
along. I'm a ditz. Everything I touch turns to disas
ter. You should have left with the others."

He looked back at the fire-charred mess on th
floor and shook his head in defeat. Unable to hel
himself, he started to laugh. Making love with Trud
would never be anything but one new adventur
after another, he conceded, and he wouldn't want i
any other way.

"Stop laughing. This isn't the slightest bit funny
Ian Walker," she scolded him as he crawled onto th
bed. On all fours, he loomed over her, forcing he

back into the sheets, to lie down under him. "You should have left."

"Not in your lifetime," he vowed, most serious. "I couldn't if I wanted to. I'm hopelessly, eternally in love with a ditz who makes my life worth living. You and I are going to make love and babies and a whole new life together." He kissed her. "Through rain and snow and sleet and hail." He nibbled at her neck and was gratified to see her eyes close softly against the outside world to focus her mind on him alone. "Through floods and earthquakes and hurricanes." His lips moved lower. "Through acts of God and man-made tragedies and through every single Truly-induced disaster that comes along."

And they did.

THE EDITOR'S CORNER

There's something a little bit forbidden about this month's group of heroes. For one reason or another they seem to be exactly the wrong men for our heroines to fall in love with—but, of course, the six ladies involved do just that, unable as they are to resist the potent allure of these special LOVESWEPT men. And what they feared was forbidden fruit turns out to be necessary to their very existences!

In **TROPICAL HEAT,** LOVESWEPT #432, Patt Bucheister creates a noble hero named John Canada, and she puts his nobility to the test by having him fight his overwhelming passion for Salem Shepherd, the woman he'd first known as a young girl. Together they had escaped from an orphanage and forged a friendship based on trust and need. But the feelings that began to surface in John as Salem blossomed into womanhood scared him, tempted him, thrilled him—and made him realize he had to send her away. Years later Salem returns to help John when his business is in trouble, and the feelings he'd once felt for her pale in comparison to the desire he knows he can no longer fight. These two people who've shared so much find themselves swept away on a current stronger than an ocean surge, right into the arms of destiny. Patt has outdone herself in crafting a love story of immense emotional impact.

Charlotte Hughes gives her heroine something of a dilemma in **RESTLESS NIGHTS,** LOVESWEPT #433. How can Kelly Garrett get on with her life as an independent single mom, when she discovers she's falling for Macon Bridges, a man who represents so much of what she's struggled to put behind her after her first marriage failed. Macon is the successful owner of the firm she works for; he has the tendency to want to take control and do things for her that she's just learned to do for herself; he's dedicated to his job and at times allows it to take top priority in his life. Then again, the man can charm the birds from the trees and certainly knows how to send Kelly's heart into flight! But

(continued)

once this smitten lady makes up her mind to risk it all on the sexy man who's causing her too many restless nights, it's Macon who doesn't stand a chance! Charlotte's lighthearted style makes this story pure entertainment.

TEMPESTUOUS, LOVESWEPT #434, by Tami Hoag, not only describes the feisty heroine in the book, Alexandra Gianni, but also the state of the atmosphere whenever she encounters hero Christian Atherton. The sparks do fly between the aristocratic charmer who is used to having women fall at his feet not throw him to the ground, and the lovely wildcat with the haunted eyes and determined ways of a woman who has something to hide. At first Christian sees winning Alex as a challenge, until he becomes thoroughly enchanted by the spirited woman he yearns to know all about. His wicked reputation seems in jeopardy as he longs only to soothe Alex's sorrow and shower her with tenderness. But not until Alex convinces herself she deserves to be cherished can she accept Christian's gift of love. This poignant romance features several characters from two of Tami's previous books, **RUMOR HAS IT,** #304, and **MAN OF HER DREAMS,** #331, the most notable character of which is hero Christian, whose love story you've asked Tami for in your letters. Enjoy!

Joan Elliott Pickart's **TO LOVE AND TO CHERISH,** LOVESWEPT #435, opens with a dramatic scene that won't fail to grip you. Imagine meeting a stranger in the foggy cocoon of night on a deserted beach. In a moment of yearning desperation, imagine yourself surrendering to him body and soul, then running off without ever learning his name! Heroine Alida Hunter was lost in her grief until she met the man with the summer-sky eyes. But she knew he was a fantasy, a magical gift she could never keep. Paul-Anthony Payton couldn't forget the mysterious woman who'd bewitched him then vanished, and he vowed to find her. She'd filled him with hope that night on the beach, but when he finally does find her, his hopes are dashed by her denial of what they'd shared.

(continued)

Alida's fear of loving and losing terrifies her and prevents her from believing in Paul-Anthony's promises. But the more she tells herself he's the forbidden lover of her dreams, the more Paul-Anthony makes her dreams become reality. Once again Joan delivers a powerful love story LOVESWEPT fans will treasure.

Judy Gill casts another memorable character in the role of hero in **MOONLIGHT MAN,** LOVESWEPT #436. Judy orchestrates perfectly this romance between Sharon Leslie, a gifted musician in whose heart the music has all but died, and Marc Duval, a man who's endured an unbearable tragedy and learned to find beauty and peace in the music he plays. Marc sees how Sharon is drawn to and yet tormented by the melodies he sends to her on the wind—as she is to his mesmerizing kisses. He knows she doubts herself as a woman even as he awakens her to pleasure beyond anything she's ever known. But until he can earn Sharon's trust, he can't know why she keeps turning away from him—and once she does trust him, he realizes he will have to confess the black secret of his own past. Caught up in the rebirth of the music inside her, Sharon revels in her feelings for Marc, but it all comes crashing down on her when she discovers the truth about the man she now loves with all her heart. Judy gives us a shining example of how true love conquers all in this wonderfully touching romance.

Fayrene Preston continues her SwanSea Place series with **JEOPARDY,** LOVESWEPT #437. Judging by the hero's name alone, Amarillo Smith, you can expect this to be one sultry, exciting, dangerous romance that only Fayrene can write—and you won't be disappointed. Heroine Angelica DiFrenza is surprised and intrigued when private investigator Amarillo, her brother's partner, asks her to dinner—the broodingly handsome detective had always seemed to avoid her deliberately. But when they finally end up alone together, the passion flares hotter than a blast furnace, and they both realize there's no going back. Amarillo couldn't deny
(continued)

what he'd felt for so long, but the time wasn't right. He was desperate to protect Angelica from the danger that threatened her life, and he needed a clear head and un-involved emotions to do it. But Amarillo's tantalizing kisses create a fever in Angelica's blood and the maelstrom of uncivilized hunger they'd suspected brewed between them rages out of control. You'll want to follow these two along on their journey of discovery, which, of course, leads them to beautiful SwanSea Place.

We promised you more information about our LOVESWEPT hotline, and here it is! If you'd like to reach your favorite LOVESWEPT authors by phone, all you have to do is dial 1-900-896-2505 between October 1 and December 31 to hear exciting mes-sages and up-to-the-minute information. You *may* call and get the author in person! Not only will you be able to get the latest news and gossip, but just by calling and leaving your name you will be entered into our Romantic Getaway Sweepstakes, where you'll have a chance to win a grand prize of a free week for two to Paris! Each call you make will cost you 95¢ per min-ute, and winners of the contest will be chosen at random from the names gathered. More detailed in-struction and rules will appear in the backs of our November, December, and January LOVESWEPTs. But the number will be operational beginning on October 1 and ending on December 31!

Get your dialing fingers ready!

Sincerely,

Susann Brailey

Susann Brailey
Editor
LOVESWEPT
Bantam Books
666 Fifth Avenue
New York, NY 10103

FOREVER
LOVESWEPT

FOREVER LOVESWEPT
SPECIAL KEEPSAKE EDITION OFFER
SELECTION FORM

Choose from these special Loveswepts by your favorite authors. Please write a 1 next to your first choice, a 2 next to your second choice. Loveswept will honor your preference as inventory allows.

$\heartsuit$ $\heartsuit$ $\heartsuit$ *Loveswept*®

_____BAD FOR EACH OTHER   Billie Green

_____NOTORIOUS   Iris Johansen

_____WILD CHILD   Suzanne Forster

_____A WHOLE NEW LIGHT   Sandra Brown

_____HOT TOUCH   Deborah Smith

_____ONCE UPON A TIME...GOLDEN

   THREADS   Kay Hooper

Attached are 15 hearts and the selection form which indicates my choices for my special hardcover Loveswept "Keepsake Edition." Please mail my book to:

NAME:_____

ADDRESS:_____

CITY/STATE:_____ZIP:_____

Offer open only to residents of the United States, Puerto Rico and Canada. Void where prohibited, taxed, or restricted. Allow 6 - 8 weeks after receipt of coupons for delivery. Offer expires January 15, 1991. You will receive your first choice as inventory allows; if that book is no longer available, you'll receive your second choice, etc.

THE SHAMROCK TRINITY

☐ **21975 RAFE, THE MAVERICK**
   by Kay Hooper $2.95

☐ **21976 YORK, THE RENEGADE**
   by Iris Johansen $2.95

☐ **21977 BURKE, THE KINGPIN**
   by Fayrene Preston $2.95